Spirit
of the Rainbow Dragon

For Riley Irungu, the 'Straightener'

One

A bird-like voice was calling shrilly.
Karo-karo. Ki!! Ki! Ki!
Karo-karo. Ki! Ki! Ki!

"Who calls?" Grandmother Rakeli wondered.

She was a very old woman, who was now a little hard of hearing. Next to her, her grandson Karoki kindled the fire. It burst into flames—a yellow dance.

"It's a bird," Karoki said mischievously, for he knew that it was his friend, Mwenda, calling.

"A strange bird it must be," his grandmother mused. "Never heard such a bird before," she added, stretching her hands over the fire for warmth.

"Yes, a strange bird," Karoki said.

Karoki was fourteen years old. He lived in Nairobi but was now visiting his grandmother in the village as he waited to proceed into high school. It was a long time since he had stayed in the village for an extended period. The last time he was in the village, he had come to help bury his grandfather and namesake. Burying his grandfather had been a sad experience, and Karoki hadn't had any time to make friends. But now he was happy. He had made some friends, and his grandmother doted on him. She called him her husband because he was named after her late husband. That made Karoki feel special. If he didn't have to go back to school, Karoki would have been happy to stay in the village forever. It was such fun.

Mwenda was calling again, imitating a bird as only he could:

Karo-karo. Ki! Ki! Ki! Ki!
Karo-karo. Ki! Ki! Ki! Ki!

"I don't like that bird. It sounds eerie. It must be a bad omen. I like birds that chime and sing like a harp," grandmother said. "Like the Red-Eyed Dove," she added with a toothless smile.

Karoki laughed. Grandmother loved that song. Even in her advanced old age, she still could not resist a good song-dance. "You're superstitious, Grandma!" chided Karoki good-humoredly.

"So I am?" Grandmother retorted. "Well, superstition has not killed me these almost one-hundred years!" She laughed.

Nobody really knew how old grandmother Rakeli was. She maintained she was going on a hundred years old. However, Mzee Gatama, who was the oldest man in the village, swore on his walking staff that she was much older. They had grown up together in the village. Mzee insisted that Rakeli was already a marriageable girl when he was but a strapping boy of about fourteen. "Otherwise, I would have married her," he would add with a naughty, toothless grin. "She was the most beautiful girl in the village!"

Grandmother Rakeli was highly respected in the village. Everybody called her Grandmother. The young women who she respectfully called *her mothers* took turns drawing water from the river and fetching firewood for her. They made sure the fire never went out in her hearth.

Karo-karo. Ki! Ki! Ki! Ki!

"Go chase that eerie bird away. It's spooky . . . and getting on my nerves!" Grandmother crossly said.

"Happily, grandmother!" Karoki said. He loved his grandmother and he didn't mind staying with her, but this Friday morning, he was a little restless. He found the prospect of spending the whole day at home a little daunting. He itched for some adventure.

"Let me chase the bird away," he called back as he dashed out of the house.

"Yes," Grandmother said. "And tell it never to come back here again!"

Meanwhile, Mwenda was roosting in the big mango tree in the garden. He was eating a huge, succulent mango—pecking on it like a bird. He too was fourteen, and although a class behind Karoki, the two boys got on well. Mwenda had an ever-restless air about him. His mind always teemed with things for them to do. When he looked at you, his small intelligent eyes seemed to swing on his narrow bird-like face, looking this way and that as though constantly on the lookout for something. It was because of this and the way he could imitate almost every bird in the forest that he had earned his nickname of Nyoni—the bird.

"Nyoni, bird of bad omen!" Karoki hailed his friend, laughing. "Stop that chirping of yours," he admonished. "You're spooking my grandmother with your ghostly call."

"Oh, I know," Mwenda said with a smile. "How is she?"

"She's fine," Karoki said. "Seems to be growing younger with every passing day."

"Good," Mwenda said. "I have always been in love with that girl, swear!"

Karoki laughed. "Well, she doesn't feel the same about you. Sorry," he said. "Actually, I'm under instructions to chase you away."

"Too bad then," Mwenda said laughing. "But I'm not surprised. A bird that perches on one tree for too long risks inviting dangers!"

As agile as a monkey Mwenda slid down the tree holding his mango in his mouth. Mwenda offered Karoki a bite. With a wave of the hand Karoki declined. His visit to the village had coincided with mango season, and he'd already eaten enough of the big juicy fruits to last him a lifetime.

"Catch me if you can," Mwenda said with a smirk, and started running.

With that, Mwenda flew over the fence in one leap. Karoki was not as good at jumping. So, by the time he went through the gate, Mwenda was way up the hill running towards the forest. He stopped to wait for his friend who was still lumbering up the hill. "We can also go and explore the forest," he said when Karoki caught up with him, huffing and puffing up the winding path. "We can go and hear what the birds and the animals are saying this Christmas season."

"It's not Christmas yet," Karoki gasped.

"Christmas is just around the bend, my friend."

"Alright then, let's go," Karoki said. "Anything is better than sitting at home. In any case, I've never been further than the edge of the forest."

"Oh, you don't know what you're missing. The forest is such a serene place. You literally hear your own thoughts!" Mwenda said.

"That's exactly what I need now," Karoki responded. "I hear they are about to release our Standard Eight exam results. A man needs serenity to reflect on his future," Karoki said.

A dark shadow seemed to fall on him, making his already dark face darker. "God," he grumbled sombrely and added: "I pray I'll pass!"

"Aw, don't be a spoilsport now," Mwenda said. "If you were meant to pass, you'll pass. If not, you'll fail. Its fate, man, and no amount of meditation can change anything. In any case it's too late in the day for that, anyway," Mwenda admonished. With that, he leaned over conspiratorially and said: "Let me tell you, dude. All will be well, don't worry. What we both need now is some fun—some adventure!"

Karoki looked at his friend. Mwenda was a happy-go-lucky sort of guy. It was clear he didn't care much about school. Karoki wished he could take life that easy.

"So, what's your great idea, sir?" Karoki asked.

"I want us to go explore the forest," Mwenda said, looking uphill where the forest rolled along with the gently undulating slopes, as gracefully as a galloping antelope.

Following his gaze, Karoki looked towards the mountain. With the sun peeping between its rugged peaks, Mount Kenya, which the locals called the *Mountain of God,* was beautiful and inviting.

"I guess you're right. We should have some fun," said Karoki, smiling up at the clear blue sky. "The mountain looks very beautiful today."

"Beautiful? Nothing!" Mwenda said. "It used to be even more picturesque back when I was young. Glaciers curved the valleys surrounding the summit. Sometimes I just can't help wondering where the glaciers disappeared to. They used to look so magical with the rising sun peering between the peaks like a little girl."

"Wow, like a girl?"

"Yes, man," Mwenda said laughing. "Like a shy, beautiful girl!"

The two boys hurried into the forest through increasingly steep tracks. The forest got thicker and thicker around them.

"The elders never want anybody to venture too deep into the jungle," Mwenda said after a while. "The chief says there are thugs in the forest."

"Hell, no!" Karoki gasped.

"Yes. And they are dangerous too. The chief says the thugs live in the Mau Mau caves."

"Mau Mau caves?"

"Yes, the caves that the Mau Mau freedom fighters used to live in."

"They lived in caves? Are you sure you're not making it up?"

"No, I swear," Mwenda said.

"I must admit that I'm a bit muddled up," Karoki said. "All this talk about thugs and caves and Mau Mau. What are you really saying?"

"Well, blockhead, what I'm saying is this: there are caves in the mountains as I suppose there must be in any mountain, right?"

"Right."

And in the 1950s or whenever it was they fought for independence, the Mau Mau—you know the Mau Mau?"

"Yes, the freedom fighters."

"Well, the freedom fighters used the caves as shelter from the elements and from the white man's bombs . . ."

Karoki thought for a while. He recalled a film on the Vietnamese War he had seen some while back and said, "That's understandable."

"The elders say the caves are sacred, but the thugs have desecrated and turned them into dens of inequities," Mwenda explained.

"But what would they be doing right now in the forest—those thugs?" Karoki asked.

Although they were all alone, Mwenda looked this way and that. It was as though he suspected that somebody might be eavesdropping on them. Then he looked at his friend, his eyes boring into Karoki. *Will he chicken out if I tell him about the thugs?* He wondered.

"I bet that's what we would want to find out, isn't it?" Mwenda said delicately, weighing his friend's response, still deliberating over whether or not to tell him.

"I suppose so," Karoki said. There was still a tinge of uncertainty in his voice. "But what do they say about the thugs? I mean, someone must have an idea about what they do in the forest?"

"Well, there are many stories that go around," Mwenda said ominously. "Some people say that deep in the forest, there are plantations of bhang owned by rich, powerful men. The gangs that run them are very dangerous. Other people say that those are not thugs at all. They say that they're squatters who have been living in the forest since the 1950s. Then, there's Kiongo. The dude claims to have seen the bhang plantations, and he says that the so-called squatters are dangerous outlaws. He says they guard the illicit farms. He says the men are mean—like *wicked mean*—and cruel. And they are the sort of fellows who won't think twice about putting a bullet through your medulla oblongata!"

"Gosh, that's scary!" Karoki gasped, jumping back.

"That's not all," Mwenda went on conspiratorially, "Kiongo swears on his mother's name that the thugs work in league with the chief!"

"Not many people will openly talk about these thugs," Mwenda went on. "Some will not even dream about them if they can help it. Unless, that is, they are having nightmares.

But what has always baffled me is why the chief should be so adamant that nobody should venture into the forest beyond a certain point. He claims it's for our own good, naturally, but some whisper that it's really for *his* own good."

"But if you are so suspicious of the chief, why haven't you reported the matter to the police?"

"Ask that of the birds!" Mwenda grinned. "But I love your innocence. I really do!"

As the boys trudged on in silence, the sun dappled the trees, and the trails were soft beneath their feet. And although it teemed with life, the forest was also very tranquil. Baboons played in the huge ancient trees, swinging from limb to limb and frightening the birds who, twittering noisily, took to flight in an explosion of color. Footprints and dung attested to the presence of elephants, buffaloes, and hyenas; the waste was a veritable playground for the beetles and numerous other unknown creatures of the forest.

"The forest is full of surprises," Mwenda went on after a long while. "If it's not a bomb, it might be an elephant, hyena, buffalo, or some other animal. Two years ago, a few of the boys and I went into the forest and found an abandoned bomb. We had no idea what it was. Some boys played with it. Then the blasted thing exploded in their faces."

"Oh, my God!" Karoki exclaimed in horror, covering his face with his hands as though to protect himself from the bomb. "Was anyone hurt?" He asked, his voice shaking.

"Oh, yes," Mwenda said. "One boy died. The other one was lucky. He survived, but they had to amputate his arm. The police came and mopped the forest. Several more bombs were found and detonated. I shall never forget how the police whipped us for that misadventure. They said we were lucky we were juveniles—whatever that means—otherwise, they would have thrown us in jail. You'd have thought we planted the bomb ourselves."

Karoki didn't know how long they had been walking when Mwenda suddenly veered off the trail.

Karoki stopped. "Where are you going?" he asked.

"This way to the river," Mwenda said. "I want to show you where we found the bomb."

Two

T he two boys continued down a valley. As they pressed onwards, the trail widened where elephants had pushed a broader swath through the forest. Likely, the elephants had been going to drink from the river at the time. The river wound its way to the bottom of the valley, its sparkling waters glistening in the sunlight like a silver ribbon. Mwenda suddenly froze.

"What is it?" Karoki whispered.

"Look over there," Mwenda said, pointing.

At first Karoki didn't see anything. Then he saw it: a dead elephant bull underneath a cluster of trees. The boys gingerly approached the dead, fallen giant. He was a magnificent beast. The elephant's tusks had been hacked close to the base. The two gaping wounds where the bullets had drilled into his brain were teeming with big, dark-blue flies. Under the heavy, dense eyelashes, his eyes looked like marbles in the sunlight. They had a slightly surprised look as if death had arrived too swiftly.

"Poachers?" Karoki asked.

"You bet!" Mwenda said, creeping close to the mountain of bloated flesh that had once been the elephant.

Karoki was so overwhelmed by an upwelling of indignation that for a moment, he could not say a word at all. "Those bastards," he finally burst out in impotent fury. "The bloody Godforsaken bastards!"

The boys watched the dead bull in quiet reverence. It was a shame to see such a grand animal so indecently exposed. The indignity of it—the shameless humiliation of such a majestic creature—was crushing. Unable to bear the sight anymore, Karoki decided to cover the carcass with tree branches. But the baboons and the birds did not take kindly to anybody vandalizing their turf to give the elephant a decent burial. They rallied and raised such a raucous that the forest rang with their protests. The boys shooed them off.

In the almost solemn silence that followed, the boys were able to give the bull some semblance of a decent burial. When they finished, Karoki saluted the leafy grave and said: "Till we meet again."

"Where do you plan to meet?" Mwenda laughed.

"In heaven. Where else?" Karoki said.

"Well, I wouldn't be surprised if somebody told me elephants go to heaven," Mwenda said. "They are so intelligent. Do you know that they actually mourn their dead?"

"You don't say!" Karoki responded.

"Yes, they do," Mwenda said. "I have never witnessed it myself, but the old men in my village say that elephants will always return to where one died, to mourn him."

"That must mean they understand life and death?"

"I suppose so."

Karoki was bemused. He said after a while, "I think human beings are the worst bigots ever. We think that we are better and more intelligent than any other creature, but are we really? Just think about it. Who except a human being will kill for greed? Animals don't kill unless they have to and then only because they have to eat or, maybe, they feel threatened and have to protect themselves. But human beings . . . Look the things we do to each other."

"I didn't know you were a sage," Mwenda laughed. "But you're right. I think heaven will basically be a zoo! Maybe there will be a few human saints like your grandma, but that's about all."

"Spit!" Karoki cried. "Spit out those words."

"Aw, what is it now?"

"I never *ever* want to imagine the day that grandma will leave us," Karoki said, deadly serious.

"Oh, I see," Mwenda said. He spat.

Afterward, when they resumed their journey up the river, the boys were strangely quiet. Their encounter with the dead elephant had produced a sobering effect on them. Each one seemed to be lost in his own thoughts. They followed the meandering river around the bend. The water trickled down into the first small waterfall and over a series of cascades before plunging down the most splendid falls Karoki had ever seen. Foamy at first, the water turned into a white spray on hitting the pool below. Then the water burst into a kaleidoscope of color, painting an arching rainbow over the rocks. A group of alligators was idly sprawling across the rocks, sunning themselves. After the ugliness of the butchered elephant, the rumbling falls was a calming sight, almost heavenly in its beauty.

"We are almost at the first cave," Mwenda said. "That's where we found that bomb I was telling you about."

Karoki didn't speak. He didn't seem to have heard. He was still savouring the beauty of the scene before them. The sun was climbing towards the noontide mark. A few high fliers surveyed the pulsing forest from regal heights while closer to the ground; other birds flapped across the river, gallivanting and ever-cheerful—their silky songs melding with the splash and hum of the river in one harmonious, ceaseless song.

Mwenda noticed the almost-ecstatic look in his friend's eyes. "It's sheer magic, yeah?" he said, happy that Karoki seemed to be enjoying the outing.

"Unbelievable. Such beauty!" Karoki said and gaped.

"I know," Mwenda laughed. He added tantalisingly, "In the village, they call this the Pool of the Rainbow Dragon . . ."

"A dragon in the river?" Karoki cringed. "Are you really sure there's a dragon in the river? I thought dragons were Chinese."

"Well . . . Mwenda said. "Let me just say that there used to be one. I really don't know the story . . ."

"What do you mean, you don't know the story?"

"It was a long time ago," Mwenda said, dreamily. "They say a severe drought ravaged our land. The people were in ferment, almost in open rebellion against their elders. The elders decided to appease the rainbow dragon and plead for rain . . ."

"Interesting," Karoki said. "How, pray, do you appease a dragon?"

"The elders offered it a sacrifice of a goat and a honey beer," Mwenda said.

"And did the bribe work? Did the rains come?"

"Aw, man, you're such a cynic. A sacrifice is not a bribe."

Karoki shrugged indifferently and Mwenda continued, "Well, as usual, the rainbow dragon rose out of the water to indulge himself. When it had eaten its fill and drunken all the beer, it started to doze off."

"It was stoned and bloated, then. All that beer and meat, I guess?"

"I suppose you're right. And so were the elders. Before they knew what was happening, some lad, *the Straightener*, they call him, crawled in on the intoxicated creature and plucked the magical hairs off its tail. Now, the dragon was the totem for the elders' power. With its magical power lost, the elders also lost authority in our community. That's how power shifted to a new generation—the Dragon generation. My grandfather, my namesake, was of this generation."

"I am not surprised the elders were overthrown," Karoki said.

"But it's a convoluted story, and I still don't know the half of it," Mwenda added. "Maybe you should ask your grandmother to tell you the story. What I know is that this is regarded as a sacred place. We weren't even supposed to come here, but we just couldn't help stealing out for a swim. That's how we discovered the caves."

With a wary eye, the alligators watched the boys' approach. Then, they scrambled into the pool, hiding. SPLASH, SPLASH, SPLASH!

Mwenda continued speaking. "When I was young, even a full-grown man couldn't get into the river without risking being swept away. It was very big and volatile," he wistfully said as the last of the reptiles disappeared downstream. With that, Mwenda removed his shoes and waded into the river, beckoning for Karoki to follow him. "Come on, man," he urged when he saw that Karoki was reluctant to follow. "Those alligators are completely harmless," he said with a laugh.

Karoki gasped when he stepped into the river. The water was cutting cold. Underneath the overarching rocks, the rushing water had chiselled a tunnel into the banks of the river. The narrow tunnel opened into a cave in the bowel of the valley and branched into different pathways. The cave was a perfect natural bunker. Karoki was surprised to see his friend produce a small flashlight. "You had it all planned out, then?" he marvelled.

"Yeah, man," Mwenda said. "I didn't want you to go back to the city before seeing these caves."

Following the narrowest of the corridors, Mwenda led the way. "I hope you're not the queasy type," he said as the corridor gave way to an ever bigger, comfy cave.

"Queasy, why?"

"You'll see why in a minute," Mwenda said. He shined his light in one of the corners.

"See that?"

"What?"

Then he saw it. Karoki almost jumped out of his skin. Etched in the wall of the cave was a skeletal fossil that looked distinctly human. Suddenly, the cave felt like it was crawling with old spirits, spirits of dead and long-forgotten men.

"He was one of the Mau Mau fighters," Mwenda sombrely said. "Imagine he has been here since the 1950s!"

"By God!"

"It's sad, isn't it?"

"Yeah, very sad," Mwenda agreed.

"Sometimes, I can't help thinking that he might be my grandfather . . ."

"Oh, no!"

Ever since he first stumbled upon the skeleton, Mwenda had never been able to shake off the feeling that it might belong to his grandfather who had disappeared in the forest during the Mau Mau war. Mwenda had once heard that his grandfather and a band of fighters had been in the vicinity of the village the night before the white man bombed the caves. Some people said that the fighters had actually been killed in the caves. Others said no, the fighters had escaped and fled to Ethiopia.

Mwenda sighed. "You know, my grandfather disappeared just like that. Like the dragon which was never heard of again after that boy plucked its tail."

Karoki was still scrutinizing the skeleton, with eyes wide open in shock. "It's a screaming scandal," he finally said.

"Yes, it screams to high heavens," Mwenda agreed. "Imagine his family not knowing where he is, and all those years he has just been lying here, forgotten and unknown!"

Karoki didn't speak. He simply didn't know what to say. So, the boys moved on in silence. Karoki was intrigued when he saw that the cave had several chambers. It seemed that at the dawn of time, when God created the world and everything in it, He must have created the caves with the express purpose of providing shelter for the gallant freedom fighters.

"Oh, damn!" Karoki suddenly cried. He had just tripped on something and was tumbling downwards.

"What is it?" Mwenda said, spinning around on his heels just in time to catch his friend before he went down, headlong. Mwenda shined the flashlight along the ground and saw something that looked like a hide skin.

"Another skeleton, maybe?" Karoki said.

The boys anxiously dug out the hide, looking to see if there might be another skeleton underneath. It looked like a loin skirt.

"Probably belonged to your grandfather, eh?" Karoki said.

"Yeah, probably."

The boys were about to give up on the digging when they unearthed a sheath. Like the loincloth, it was made up of tough buffalo hide. And inside the sheath was the greatest find of the day: a gun.

"A gun?" Mwenda cried, not believing his eyes.

"Looks like it!"

Excited, the boys scrambled out of the cave to examine their surprise find in the brighter light of the sun. They splashed across the river but when they clambered across to the bank, their shoes were missing!

Mwenda was more surprised than alarmed. "This is strange," he said.

"Somebody stalking us?"

"Looks like it."

"Who would it be?"

"No idea. The poachers maybe."

"Could it be the thugs?"

"Poachers or thugs, they're both the same—dangerous," Mwenda said. "But the thugs are supposed to be deep in the forest. We've hardly left the village."

"We have been walking for a long time," Karoki said doubtfully. "The village must be way, way behind us."

Mwenda shrugged indifferently. He was still examining the gun. It was made up of hard, polished wood with a metal barrel. The trigger was a bit rusty and crusted with soil.

"Let's pray this thing works," he said.

"It needs to be thoroughly cleaned," Karoki said.

Mwenda fetched a penknife from his pocket and proceeded to peel off the rust from the gun.

"It seems to be in surprisingly good condition after all those years," Karoki observed. "I hope it's in working condition."

"I'll wash it in the river."

"No, dude. That's the surest way to ruin it," Karoki said. "What you need is a spirit to remove the rust for you. And oil. A gun must be oiled for optimum performance."

"You're nuts. Where can one find such a thing in the jungle?" Mwenda said. "But I have an idea," he added.

"Yes?"

Mwenda grinned. He unzipped his trousers and turned to face the other way.

"What are you up to, man?"

"I'm improvising," Mwenda said. "Urine is as good as any spirit. I'm sure it can remove the rust. It's corrosive enough, aye?"

"You sure are a true village bumpkin, my friend!"

"No, a village genius," Mwenda laughed. "In the village, we know how to innovate!"

Then, he fetched a rough stone from the river and used it to scrape the rust off of the gun. "See," he said, holding up the gun, proudly. "The urine works. In fact, it's better than any spirit."

"Well, I suppose as long as what needs to be done gets done . . ."

"You're right!" Mwenda said, still laughing. "Would you know how to use the gun? I've never handled a gun, myself," he said.

"I've never used one, either," Karoki admitted and quickly added, "But it should not be hard for me."

"How come?"

"I bet I've watched enough movies to know how to use a gun," Karoki said. "Here, let me give it a try."

"But you don't have any bullets," Mwenda said, handing Karoki the gun.

"No problem. I just want to see whether its mechanics are still intact."

Karoki turned dramatically, sweeping one leg along the ground, and going down on one knee in the same way as the movie stars. He pointed the gun at his friend and said, "Say your last prayers, dude, before I bang you up to the next world!"

Feigning fear and panic, Mwenda lifted his arms up. "Don't shoot, buddy!" he cried and dove to the ground just as Karoki pulled the trigger. He was just in time. Against all expectations, the gun discharged.

BANG!!

Karoki watched in horror as the bullet whizzed just over Mwenda's head and embedded itself in a tree trunk with a dull *thud*. The birds squawked and took to the air in a frenzy.

"Jesus of Nazareth!" Karoki cried, dropping the gun as though it had suddenly turned scalding hot in his hand. His jaw nearly fell to the ground. His hand was shaking. Then, his whole body was quivering like he had suffered a massive nervous attack.

Mwenda lay flat and buried his face in the undergrowth. The ground smelt thick with mould. He rarely prayed unless he was in trouble. Now he said a silent prayer, thanking Mary Mother of Christ for interceding for him and saving him from an ignominious death. The forest was deathly quiet.

"Gosh," he slowly said when he finished, "Gosh, that was way too close!"

"I'm so sorry," Karoki said. "I-I didn't mean to . . ."

He looked at his friend. The expression on Mwenda's face was indescribable. It was the expression of a man who had just come face to face with the horrors of the netherworld.

"I know," Mwenda said. "But it was still too close for comfort, man!"

"I would never for the life of me have suspected that the accursed thing was loaded. God is my witness!" Karoki said.

Mwenda grinned and jumped to his feet. "Okay," he said, "Lick your nose if you tell the truth."

Karoki tried, but of course his tongue couldn't reach his nose.

"You see, you lie!" Mwenda charged. He strode towards his friend. Fearing the worst, Karoki readied himself for a fight. But then, Mwenda offered him his hand. The two boys shook hands and bumped shoulders. There were tears in Karoki's eyes.

"Take it easy," Mwenda said. "I believe you, Karo-ki-ki-ki!" He added, making light of the situation. He picked up the gun. "Wonder, could it have any more bullets by any chance?"

When they checked, the boys found out that the gun had four more bullets. With an expansive gesture, Mwenda threw open his arms as if he was going to embrace the forest.

"Well, step out now if you're on our trail. We're ready for you!" he called to the woods.

Mwenda seemed to have finally recovered from the scary experience. But his words reminded Karoki that somebody was supposedly trailing them.

Karoki murmured, "They would be from the plantations, don't you think?"

"Maybe. Maybe not," Mwenda said. "Frankly, to tell the truth, I'm not sure I ever believed the story about thugs growing bhang in the forest. It always sounded like a tall tale—an ogre kind of story, meant to keep prying eyes away from the forest."

"But why bother?"

Mwenda explained about how not so long ago, the forest used to be almost impenetrable. Then loggers and incendiary charcoal dealers arrived.

"They cart off lorryfuls of forest to I-don't-know-where. I have a feeling the chief is in league with the illegal loggers who have been desecrating the forest for years," he said. "I think that's why he doesn't like people coming into the forest.

He doesn't want people to discover his secret. He says it's a protected area, whatever that means."

"Apparently it doesn't mean much," Karoki said, stopping to look at where a whole lot of trees had been cut, leaving only the stumps jutting out from the undergrowth. "But surely there must be forest officers charged with the responsibility of preventing this kind of wanton destruction? This will have dire consequences for the future," he said.

"Well, the future is already here with us, if you ask me," Mwenda muttered. "The Mountain is dying. The rivers are drying up, and the seasons are no longer what they used to be," he sombrely added.

Then Mwenda, who was leading the way, suddenly stopped in his tracks. He put a finger to his lips. "Silence," he whispered. As Karoki came level with him, Mwenda pointed up a tree.

"What is it?" Karoki whispered.

Looking up, he saw a leopard arched on a branch just above them, perfectly camouflaged by the leaves and the speckled shade. Karoki gasped. His hair stood on edge, and his body broke out in goose pimples. His heart was racing, fit to burst. The big cat above them fixed its big fiery eyes on the boys and softly snarled. *Keep your distance,* the eyes warned.

"Oh, my! This is dangerous!"

"Dangerous? Nothing," Mwenda said, back to his old self again. "A leopard is a shy animal and is very secretive. It'll normally not bother you if you don't bother it."

So, the boys detoured, dodging the tree on which the leopard was perched. The leopard's growl followed them. When they had gone some safe distance, Karoki turned to his friend and said, "Man, I nearly freaked out!"

Mwenda shrugged. "The old man was just afraid we might snatch his snack."

"His snack?"

"Yes. He had a kill up there in the tree. Some hapless dik, I think. You didn't notice?"

"No. But say, how did you know he's a male?" he asked.

"He's a big and stocky fellow. Females are much smaller and less colorful," Mwenda said. "But as I said, leopards will not attack. They'd always rather steal away. What I fear is the buffalo. A lone old bull will attack without the slightest provocation—even trail or ambush you. He's the most dangerous animal in the bush. And, man, he's a demon with daggers on his head!"

"I never expected to see a leopard at this altitude," Karoki said. "Leopards on Mount Kenya? Man, I can hardly believe it!"

"I suppose a lot of people think it's a myth because sightings are very rare," Mwenda said. "But there you are—or would like to go back, to confirm?"

"Hell, no!" Karoki cried.

The boys' light banter was suddenly shattered by what sounded like the clap of a whip. It was followed by the shrill, anguished cry of a woman in distress. In the silence of the forest, her voice reached the boys with sharp, rasping echoes. It was as if the impassive jungle itself was mocking her.

Mwenda dove to the ground and started crawling for the cover of a nearby bush. Karoki followed. The two lads hid in the thick undergrowth and waited, tense and alert. The woman's cries grew nearer and nearer. Then, she was within sight.

Mwenda recognized the girl at once.

Three

The girl before them was around twenty and easily the most beautiful girl in Hombe village. She was in a simple floral dress with a lesso tied across her middle. For Mwenda and his peers, it was a matter of great regret that they were still too young to talk to her in that special way they all secretly desired. To be sure, the girl was polite and unassuming, almost to a fault. She had that rare talent of making all, young or old, feel special in her presence. But that was deceptive for many—not least the local chief, who had learned that beneath the modest demeanour was a girl of steely pride who didn't suffer fools gladly. And now, here she was—Mumbi, the village beauty—deep in the forest with a strange whip-swinging man!

The man's face was covered with a hideous bandana. In one hand he carried two pairs of shoes, strung together by a single lace. And in the other hand, he brandished a lash.

"Move," he growled and swung the whip. "I don't have all day!"

The girl screamed as the leather whip connected and coiled itself around her legs like a snake. Then, the man extracted and swung the whip again. It unfurled above his head, hissing like a viper, ready to strike again.

Mwenda shuddered. *Stop it!* He screamed at the man inside his heart.

"You should kill me," the girl hissed, her voice dripping with contempt. "You should just go ahead and kill me!"

The whip connected again. She let out a wild scream, lurching backwards.

"What's going on?" Karoki whispered.

"I think that she has been kidnapped!"

"Yeah, but even so, what kind of a man strikes a girl like that?"

"A man? My foot!"

"Heck, I won't cover here and watch him torment the poor girl any longer, whatever he is!"

"Yeah, we need to do something."

Karoki looked back up at the kidnapper. He was a hulk of a man, over six feet tall, dressed in an old police jacket, with a machete on his belt. For a moment, Karoki thought that the man was a policeman, a forest officer, or maybe even a game ranger. But the man looked rough and a wee bit too unkempt—more like a member of a drug-inundated bush militia than a member of any disciplined force. In any case, why would an officer need to wear a hood like some deranged terrorist?

"I think if we attack swiftly and surprise him, we might be able to disarm him and free the girl," Mwenda whispered.

The viper struck again. The girl screamed, keeling over, sunk down into the ground.

"The gun . . ."

"Oh, yes, the gun," Karoki said. "I forgot all about it!"

"I'll shoot the goon!"

Karoki looked up, with eyes wide and full of fear. "No, don't. He's more useful alive than dead. Besides, this might be our only chance to find out if the forest gangs do indeed exist. In any case, you don't want them to send you off to juvenile jail for murder, do you?"

"I don't care," Mwenda said, seething. "He's a vile monster. He should be erased from the face of the earth."

"No," Karoki said. "That's exactly what they'll do if you shoot him, dude—pack you off to the cooler. You're not allowed to take the law into your hands, you know?"

"Nonsense!"

"The law is an ass," Karoki said. "That's how it is, and there is nothing to be done."

"Then the jailer has some waiting to do," Mwenda said. "As long as beautiful girls like Mumbi walk these hills, I don't plan on going to anybody's jail," he added with a sly grin.

"You know her, then?"

"You ought to know her, too. She's one of your grandma's best friends. Besides, she's adorable."

Karoki recognized the girl, just then. He looked closer, realising that he had seen her at his grandmother's home several times and had been struck by her pure, natural beauty. He felt his whole body cringe as the whip cracked again. The girl let out an anguished cry. Flailing and screaming, she fought back like a wild cat as the man tried to lift her back up to her feet.

Karoki crossed himself, muttering under his breath. "Hail Mary, full of Grace . . ." Then, without warning, he swung into action. He was like an enraged buffalo as he charged at the man. The hooded man turned around as Karoki came up behind him. The goon was surprisingly swift, but his nemesis was already airborne. Karoki unleashed a savage flying kick. His packed heel connected with the goon's bulky chest and threw him back against the stump of a stinkwood tree. The man gasped. He dropped the shoes and the whip flew out of his flailing hand as he tried to stop himself from keeling over. As he sunk to his knees, Karoki fell upon the thug, raining blow after blow.

Mumbi jumped up to her feet. She was crying, and her whole body was throbbing with pain. The pain made her recklessly wild. She clawed at the man, tearing off the woollen hood and drawing blood. But the man was no pushover, either. Growling like some primal beast, his blood-shot eyes flared with a murderous rage. His hand a blur, like the dart of a chameleon's tongue, the man whipped the machete from his belt. Mumbi involuntary closed her eyes as the man lunged.

Then . . .

"Drop that machete. Or I'll put a bullet through your brain. That's if you have one, you stupid baboon!"

It was like a voice from above. Mumbi opened her eyes to see Mwenda emerge like a ghost, out of a bush, gun at the ready. Was the gun real?

The answer was in the goon's strawberry eyes. They widened and widened some more as Mwenda stepped forward, gun drawn. Terror swiftly replaced anger in the man's eyes as Mwenda cocked the weapon.

This show had taken on a different twist. Mumbi stepped aside to watch the drama unfold. The man let the machete drop at his feet and lifted his hands.

"As you say, chief," he grinned.

Chief.

It was all Mumbi could do to keep from throwing up. So disgusted was she. She looked at Mwenda. He looked self-assured—almost cocky. She smiled at him, and he saw the plea in her eyes. Don't shoot, they said. Mwenda smiled back at her and winked. No, I won't shoot. I'm just bullying the guy, his eyes said. Mumbi was relieved.

"Alright," Mwenda said to the thug. "Now go down—down on your face!"

"You won't shoot, brother?"

"That's up to me, isn't it?"

"You won't let him shoot, please?" The man said to Mumbi.

"Down!" Mwenda yelled.

The man went down and buried his face in the ground. The boys used his belt to tie the man's hands behind his back. Karoki took the double-edged machete and felt the two blades with his finger. He had not the slightest doubt that the man, like some gladiator of yore, would have impaled him on the machete in an instant, had he made the wrong move and not been so lucky. For a moment, Karoki wished that he was living in a different age: a time when the law was a distant dream and justice was swift and clinical. After all, a man who kidnapped a girl and whipped her so mercilessly . . . a man who would kill you without a second thought deserved no less. He deserved to be hewn like a carcass only fit for the hounds!

"These are our shoes, alright," Mwenda said, taking the shoes away from the man's belongings. "Say, why did you take our shoes?" he asked the goon.

"I didn't know they were yours," the man said, with his face still pressed up against the ground.

"Who did you think they belonged to? Or did you think they germinated from the ground like mushrooms?"

"I didn't think that," the man said. "I thought maybe the owners had been eaten by wild beasts or maybe they had drowned in the river. Then I thought, why waste good shoes? So, I took them."

The man spoke dispassionately. It was as if a person being killed by wild animals or drowning in the river was for him a trifling matter, and he could not be bothered.

"You sure are a fine specimen of a man!" Karoki said, sarcastically. Then, he turned to Mwenda, who was still putting on his shoes, "What are you supposed to do with a guy who hopes that you'd be killed by wild animals? A man who would enjoy it if you drowned in the river?"

Mwenda passed Karoki's shoes to him and grinned. "If you promise not to flaunt the law in my face, I'll tell you the answer," he said. "It's a no-brainer, really. In fact, I have a mind to . . . you know, give him a taste of his own medicine, pressed down and overflowing," he added with a chuckle.

"I know, my friend," Karoki said, enjoying this. "You can use his own machete."

"No, please . . . I beg!" The man cried.

"Shut up!" Karoki hissed.

He put one foot on the man's head. He was still thinking about the machete. He imagined the metal cutting through flesh and solid bone and cringed. Mwenda joined him. Together they posed, like hunters posing with the trophy of an animal they had felled.

"Thank you, brother," Karoki said, emotionally.

"Yeah?"

"You probably saved my life," Karoki said. "The goon was going to cut me down, no doubt."

"And you guys saved *my* life," Mumbi said.

"I wouldn't kill a lady," the man mumbled.

"You wouldn't?" Karoki sneered. "Of course, you wouldn't. You'd inflict pain which would be much worse than death."

"No, not me—the devil . . ."

"Oh, keep the devil out of this!" Mwenda said. He turned to Mumbi: "You were born under a lucky star, beauty!"

"I can't thank you enough," Mumbi said. "God bless you, two!"

"That's all right," Mwenda said. "But why don't you bless us—me—yourself?"

"Bless you like how?"

"Like give me a hug!"

Mumbi laughed. "Just that?"

"Yes. Just that," Mwenda said.

She hugged him.

Karoki opened his arms wide. "BII-G HUU-G!" he said.

Mumbi hugged him, too.

"So how did you find yourself with the goon?" Mwenda asked.

"I was fetching firewood for grandma Rakeli when he pounced on me," Mumbi said. Her hands flew to cover her face as she relived the horror of the moment. "I dread to imagine what would have become of me if you guys hadn't happened along," she said.

"I'm so glad you're safe," Karoki said.

"It was quite an ordeal. I was so scared," Mumbi said with feeling. It was clear that the encounter with the goon had traumatized her.

"Well, some good came out of it in the end." Mwenda smiled mischievously. "I got a hug!"

"Silly boy!" Mumbi said, laughing.

***

"Now, what do we do with the ruffian?" Karoki asked.

"There's only one thing that I know for sure," Mwenda said.

"What?"

"We can't just let him go free!" Mwenda declared.

"Agreed!" Mumbi said.

"Can we take him to the police station?" Karoki asked.

"Oh, what a killjoy!" Mwenda protested.

He turned to the man and ordered him to sit up. With his hands tied behind his back, it was a struggle to sit up at all. Mwenda pointed the gun at him. "I'll close my eyes," he slowly said. "I'll count up to five, and if you're not seated by the time I finish, you'll lie on the ground forever or until the predators turn you into carrion!" He started to count: "One . . . two . . ." The man struggled. ". . . Three . . . four. Hurry up!" Mwenda said, kicking the man in the backside. "We don't have all day."

The man finally managed to sit up. He slumped against a tree, a woe-be-gone expression on his face.

"Good," Mwenda said. "Now, tell me, who are you? Do you work in the bhang plantations by any chance?"

"What bhang plantations?" the man retorted. "I have no idea what you're talking about."

"Is that how you're going to talk to me?" Mwenda demanded.

"The guy is quite rude," Karoki said. "Are you sure you don't know of any bhang plantations in the forest?" he asked the man.

"Yes, sure," the man said, looking down at his weather-beaten military boots. One of them had a gaping tear in the heel. It reminded Karoki of a yawning alligator.

"But you're a kidnapper all the same. Aren't you? Do you have any idea how much worse a crime that is? After all, you've proven yourself to be a kidnapper, a monster—a woman eater. That will surely excite the police. Some judge will be all too happy to send you to the gallows—and with a clear conscience too, I promise!"

"It's not me, brother," the man pleaded. "It's the devil."

"The devil? What about him?"

"Yes, the devil. Every time he comes to the forest . . ."

"The devil comes to the forest?" Mumbi asked incredulously.

"Yes," the man said. "And every time he comes, we have to find women for him."

"I suppose like some kind of human sacrifice. Is that it?" Karoki sneered. "Well, we'll see what the law makes of that!"

"Can't we just keep the law out of this, brothers?"

"Of course, we can," Mwenda said. "I don't like the law either. It's an ass. I'd very much prefer you to deal with our villagers. I guarantee you this: they'll be very pleased to send you off to your maker in a blaze of glory, on a splendid log fire!"

"Oh, no!" The man cried, horrified.

Even Mumbi had to laugh. How was it that one, so quick to inflict pain could freak out so easily when threatened? It was unbelievable. Was it duplicity or was it merely shameful cowardice? Either way, the boys were having fun.

"You don't want the police. You don't want the villagers. That's the making of what we call a dilemma," Karoki said.

"Yeah, a dilemma," said Mwenda glibly. "I guess the only way out of this fix is for me to put the metal through his mouth!"

"Oh, no!" The man cried, again. "Don't shoot me, brother."

Looking at the man and seeing the horror in his eyes, Karoki learned something about the power of the gun. Once there was a gun in the equation, it tilted the scales in such a way that no matter who you were, the last thing you wanted was to have it pointed in your direction. It didn't matter whether it was an old, rusty or even malfunctional gun.

It was a revelation.

"Then you have to choose," Karoki said with a laugh. "It's either you talk to the police, the villagers, or to us. The choice is yours."

The man considered it for a while. Apparently, he wasn't much used to thinking, for his face creased with the effort.

"Alright, brothers," he said. "I'll talk—to you."

"Good. Well, we already know about the bhang plantations," Mwenda said, with a flourish. "But you'll tell us everything. What we know and what we don't know. I guess it'll be a long story, but don't you worry. We have plenty of time to hear a good story. Only that it had better be true. Otherwise . . . Anyways, it's a deal?"

"Deal."

"Now, start from the beginning," Mwenda said. "Sing. Sing like a parrot, man."

The position of the sun began lowering around noon. The shadows grew short, stunted. The forest was still. An aura of peace hung over the jungle. Karoki ordered the man to remove his boots. Mumbi involuntarily curled her lips; such was the stink from the kidnapper's feet.

His gun ready on his lap, Mwenda sat on a stump of a tree and kept a wary eye on the captive.

Then, the goon started his story . . .

Four

"Well, you asked about me," the man said. "The truth is that a certain old man ruined me . . ."

"An old man?" Mumbi asked, doubtfully.

"Yes, I fell under the spell of a certain old fabulist and the devil, that's what!"

"Alright," Karoki said softly, sure they were dealing with a crank. "But before you were ruined, you must have had a name?"

"Oh, yes. My mother called me Kahocio. Later, she took me to church and I was given the name Ignatius."

"Okay, Ignatius Kahocio," Mwenda said, gleefully. "This promises to be more interesting than I imagined. Now the story . . ."

Ignatius gulped and said: "I grew up with my mother at Mwisho wa Reli, a slum village at the end of the railway line on the fringes of Nanyuki town. You know the village on the slopes of Mount Kenya, way out on the way to Meru? Yes? Well, the older men had a story about the railway. They said that it was supposed to go all the way through Nanyuki to Isiolo and onwards to Meru. But when it got to Nanyuki, they said, there were just too many pleasures. The engineers got distracted. They lost their heads and their maps, and there was nothing to be done but terminate the line at Mwisho . . ."

"Sounds familiar," Mwenda said, reflectively.

"It might be," Ignatius said. "The story is well-known. Somebody even made a song about it, I remember."

"Yes!" Mwenda exclaimed. "Kajohnie? Was that the musician's name? You know, my father always played the song, but foolish me, I never paid much attention to it!"

"I don't remember who made the song," Ignatius said. "It's been a long time since I heard it, but you see? It's true, what I'm telling you," he added.

"That's fine. They say that the truth will set you free," Karoki chuckled. "It just might. Continue . . ."

Ignatius picked up his story . . .

"Everything would have been fine if I hadn't listened to the old man. He had arrived at Mwisho on the train from I-don't-know-where. He didn't know from where, either. He wasn't destined for our village. He didn't even know it existed. But it was at the end of the railway line, so he got off the train and settled in our village. He was a wily little man, that's for sure. He did not talk much, and I thought there was something rather sad about him. Anyway, he took a liking to me, and we became sort of friends. That's when all my troubles started . . .

"You see, the old geezer was a Mau Mau veteran. At least that's what he said. He had fought the British in the forests during the war for independence. But he had lost his land, and his wife had run off during the war, and that's enough to break a man. But when we became friends, I discovered that the old man was not all doom and gloom. He had the most incredible stories. He told me stories about Mau Mau fighters who would bring down enemy planes with homemade guns. *Homemade.* Imagine that. He told me, too, about others who could throw a machete a whole seven miles and not miss their target. He firmly believed that the Mau Mau war was never finished. He talked about a specific Mau Mau General—I forget the name—who supposedly disappeared during the war, as if by magic. He insisted the General would soon return to complete the unfinished war. Although he was ancient, the man swore he would not die before fighting in the war again, which he believed was just about to resume. And he kept a sharpened machete by his bed for the sole purpose of readying himself for the war to come. He didn't plan on getting himself a gun or anything like that, he said. His old machete would do just fine. He was dead serious, too. At the time of the coup . . ."

Ignatius paused. He looked at his sceptical audience. His eyes were moving appraisingly from one to the other. "But you guys are too young," he finally said. "You wouldn't know anything about the failed coup attempt. Would you?"

"That was in 1982?" Karoki said.

"Yes, eighty-two it was. My old friend took to the streets with his machete, singing old war songs. He thought the war he'd been waiting for was finally back on. They promptly arrested him. I don't know what they did to him in the cooler, but when he came back, he was a changed man—a recluse. And he was ill. He wouldn't let us take him to the hospital, though. No white man's medicine for him, he said. He would only allow an old Samburu medicine man to treat him with herbs. The medicine man came once a week. I used to help him treat the old man. But my old friend died shortly afterward. He just went to bed one day. The following day, when he tried to wake up, he was dead. Just like that!"

"What balderdash!" Karoki said. "Was he right in the head?"

"Who knows whether anyone is right in the head or not?"

"It's a weird story, all the same," Karoki said.

"Well, you asked for my story," Ignatius said.

"Yes, but all you're telling us about is some crazy old man," Mwenda said.

"It's just the kernel of my story. I thought you said you've got all the time?" Ignatius said and continued:

"Anyways, it was this old geezer that ruined me. You see, I used to be intrigued by the trains. The sound of the train's siren as it left Mwisho always left an aching longing inside my heart. I didn't know what I yearned for until the old man told me. Fortune, he told me, was what I was yearning for. He said, 'Fortune always favors the wayfarer.' He advised me to get on the train and go seek it. He said, 'If you don't find it at the next stop, you'll find it at the next, or the next . . .' I thought: Why not? I mean, there was nothing to do in Mwisho, and life was hard. Besides, my going would mean one less mouth for my mother to feed. So, I left. After sojourns in Nyeri, Karatina, and Sagana, I found my way to Nairobi. I was sixteen. That's how my life on the streets of the city begun. And that's where, after more than ten years of hustling on the mean Nairobi streets, I met the devil . . ."

"It's quite a long story," Karoki said.

"And that's just half of it," Ignatius said.

"Did you find your kismet in the city, then?"

"Yes, if you can call scavenging in the garbage heaps that!" Ignatius said.

"What about it, then?"

"My life changed when one day, I met the devil."

"You met who?" Mumbi shrilled.

"The devil. A hulky one-eyed fellow named Pablo."

"Sounds like a real Calypsos!" Karoki said. "But wait!" he exclaimed, remembering a film he had once watched about a Columbian drug dealer by the name Pablo. "Did you say, Pablo? Is that his real name?"

"Yes, Pablo. One of my colleagues nicknamed him the Black Devil. We simply called him the Devil or sometimes Boss," Ignatius wearily replied before resuming his story:

"He—the Devil, that is—used to visit a certain lady near our hangout in Korogocho. That woman was the undisputed Queen of the Underworld. And she was powerful. She was loaded with money and was as beautiful as the Devil was ugly. In the underworld, that's always a lethal combination in a woman—wealth, and beauty. Anyway, she and the Devil were in some kind of business. That was for sure. I didn't know which kind of business. All I know is that she made the most potent *changaa*, and her brewery down by the river had a production to rival that of any legal company you can think of. But there was another side to that lady that only a few knew. She was kind and generous. That's how my gang came to work for her, when she got us off the streets. You know, taking care of rivals—destroying a brewery here and there . . . harassing rivals' customers. Things like that. The lady liked me because I used to make a good job of it. I remember one night, she asked me to go to her house. Full of expectations, I made my way to her home on the decent side of town only to find two other husky fellows already there. As you can imagine, I was a bit disappointed. But it seemed like we were going to have a party, which was fine with me. It was a good party, too, with plenty of fine food, drinks, and music. Then sometime well past midnight, our good lady stopped the music. 'This is a good time to dispose of the body,' she said.

"Body?" Mumbi gasped.

"Yes, *body*. I looked at the other fellows. They were more perplexed than I was."

"Continue, man!" Mwenda said.

"The lady led us to her bedroom. The body was in a body bag underneath her massive bed. Well, if you allow—for the sake of our sister here—I'll just say, whoever that was, he had met a most horrendous death. Even now, I shudder to imagine how many times he must have died before he finally found release from his agony. Anyways, that's the first time I made anything close to a fortune. The lady said if I were man enough and knew how to keep my mouth shut, there would more and better-paying jobs. Then the Devil tempted me, and all was lost . . ."

Ignatius paused reflectively.

Mumbi asked the question that was on all of their minds: "This devil . . . was he the *real* devil?"

"Well, as I said, that's what we called the boss—the Black Devil. One of my colleagues gave him the name. He's a real devil, too, I swear," Ignatius said and then continued with the story:

"I was at the Queen's den when one of the regular customers turned up. Sammy Onyango was a driver with one of those Indian firms in the Industrial Area. After doing his employer's deliveries, he would pass by for a swig. Sometimes, he did deliveries for the Queen on the sly. That day, he turned up in a Toyota Hilux pickup. It was a brand-new, double-cabin black beauty. It so happened that the one-eyed Black Devil was around. It all started as a joke. Black Devil said Sammy was an idiot—just like that, straight out of the blue.

"Then, I remember what happened. 'I'm nobody's idiot, *yawa*!' Sammy protested, with his dark face turning almost blue with indignation.

" 'But you are all the same,' Black Devil insisted.

'You know, they say a monkey doesn't see his backside,' he cryptically added.

"Sammy, who had taken a bit of changaa and who knows what else, exploded. 'Who gave you the right to insult me like that? Who the hell do you think you are?'

"All through the tirade, Devil remained as calm as a monk. When Sammy exhausted himself, Devil offered to buy him a drink. Never one to turn down a bottle, Sammy accepted. 'Talk is cheap,' Devil said after Sammy had been served his drink. 'Real men don't talk too much. They do things,' he pointed out.

"Now real mellow, Sammy asked the devil: 'So, what would you have me do, My Lord, so you know I'm a real man?'

" 'That pickup truck is worth a fortune just across the border in Uganda,' Devil said. He said it so casually, nobody would have suspected the nefarious scheme that he had in mind. Then, Devil leaned forward. 'You can make yourself a tidy pile of money if you are man enough. Have you ever handled a million bob in all those years you've worked for that little Indian of yours? No? And you call yourself a man?' Devil chided. 'Listen,' he said to the crestfallen Sammy. 'Here in Nairobi, there are two types of people. There are those who come to make their fortune, and there are those who came to help them make it. So, my dear friend, Sammy, you either make it your life's mission to help that little Indian make his fortune or you take matters into your own hands and let him help you make your own fortune for a change. *Hii maisha mtu ni kujipanga*, my friend. It's as simple as that.'

"Of course Sammy had never handled a million bob. I mean, how many people could claim to have seen a million in the early nineties? The Goldenberg fellows, certainly, but those were just a few guys. The rest of us were all bleeding. The whole country was bleeding. Blood and tears. And you weren't even allowed to complain that you were hurting. Anyways, the Devil is a cunning fellow; that's for sure. Sammy was mellowing. He was coming around like a boomerang. After some back and forth, he agreed to the deal. The poor bastard. And meanwhile, I didn't know I would end up an outlaw in some godforsaken forest either, living like some wild animal . . ."

Once again, Ignatius paused. He shook his head as if to shake off the memories of those long-gone days, summoning his mind back to the present. The forest was deathly silent. A flurry of birds flew and chirped overhead. The commotion made absolutely no impression on the all-encompassing stillness of the forest, which swayed to a song all its own in the light breeze.

"So, how did you end up here?" Karoki asked.

"The Devil," Ignatius spat. "He roped me into that deal!"

"How come?" Mwenda asked.

"He said he didn't trust Sammy. He looked like a man who could easily freak out and betray everything." With that, Ignatius took a deep breath, and continued on with the story:

"Black Devil had everything figured out. I would play the role of one of the carjackers. We would rough up Sammy a bit, just to bring him up to speed with his role in the show. Once we were through with him, he would walk to the Muthaiga police station and report that he had just been robbed of the car at gunpoint. Meanwhile, one of Black Devil's henchmen and I would drive the car to Kisumo. The buyer would be waiting for us at a hotel. I forget the name. We would give him the car and collect the money and then return by train to Nairobi, where the loot would be shared.

" 'It's about as easy as that,' Black Devil said. Besides, he added, 'There's nothing to worry about. I have connections in the right places and will have your backs.'

It sounded easy enough. I was tottering on the edge of being broke. In fact, I *was* broke. And now, here was providence, smiling down on me, again. I remembered the words of the old man back home in Mwisho, telling me about how fortune always favors the wayfarer. So, I jumped at the chance."

Ignatius grinned and continued:

"My friends, it was like I was riding in an enchanted car on the drive to Kisumo. I was nervous, not with fear, but with excitement! I thought about what I'd do with the fortune I would make in the hustle. I thought about my mother back in Mwisho. Maybe, I'd buy myself a plot and build her a nice little house. I could find myself a beautiful girl and get married. Maybe . . . Maybe . . . Maybe. You could say I was counting my chicks before they'd hatched. Finally, I couldn't decide what I'd do with the loot. 'Wait until you get your share of the money', I said to myself. 'Then, go home or better still, go to some quiet place—a hotel maybe—and think properly.' One thing I knew was that this time around, I needed to be more careful with my loot. I told myself that after all those years, I must never return to Mwisho like the prodigal son. Never!"

"So, you took the car to Kisumu?"

"Of course, Godspeed! We got to Kisumo at around midnight and went straight to the hotel where we met Mugaga. That was the Ugandan who would buy the car."

"And he gave you your millions?" Mumbi prompted.

"Millions? The bastard gave us five . . ."

"Heck, no!" Karoki exclaimed. "The car couldn't fetch five million in those days, never!"

"I meant to say five thousand shillings," Ignatius smiled indulgently.

"Are you nuts? A brand-new double cabin pickup?"

Ignatius sighed deeply and continued:

"Well, the five thousand was for us to see the Lakeside town. Mugaga said we'd get the payment for the car in the morning when the banks opened. That was fair enough, we thought. So, we took the five thousand shillings and hit the town. Man, did we drink! We partied like it was Christmas. After some time, when I looked around, I suddenly couldn't find my friend. I said to myself, 'No problem. Maybe he's savouring the town's delights.' So, I carried on drinking and making merry with my nyakos —real ebony queens, those lakeside girls. Anyways, the following morning—it was nearer to noontime, actually—when I went to the hotel, they wouldn't even allow me past the gate.

" 'You want to see who? Oh, hard luck, brother. Mr. Mugaga left for Kampala last evening!' "

"What happened to your friend, the co-driver?" Karoki asked.

"He had just melted into thin air. Never saw him again," Ignatius said. "Sometimes, I think he was a phantom, not a man!"

"I think you were dumb. You were duped," Mwenda said.

"I admit that I was naïve," Ignatius agreed. "But the worst was still to come . . ."

And so, Ignatius continued his story:

"That afternoon, I had only a hundred shillings in my pocket. My head was drumming. All afternoon, I did a round of all the bars, hoping to find my friend. After a simple lunch, and now completely penniless, I had no idea how I would get back to Nairobi. I was walking in the market near the bus station when I heard somebody call my name.

" 'Homeboy, Ignatius!'

"I turned and saw my former classmate, Gachoka. Man, I've never been so happy to see a man! He was a second-hand clothes trader in Kisumo. He looked happy and contented with his life. But above all else, he seemed genuinely happy to see me. We shook hands like the good old friends we were. I weaved him a yarn: I had come to Kisumo on an official assignment, but I had missed the company car back to Nairobi. I had no money, but if he were kind enough to give me fare to Nairobi, I would send him the money immediately when I arrived in the city. He looked suspicious at first, but when I admitted that I had gotten drunk and lost all the money I had, he kind of understood."

Ignatius looked at Mumbi and grinned: "I don't mean any disrespect, but that's the difference between men and women. Men easily understand that kind of situation. A man will spare you the humiliation of having to explain everything. But a woman will drag you through the mud. And if you tell her the truth, she'll dismiss you as wretch not worth her help. So, you are forced to tell her embellished lies. Gachoka was quite generous. I very much regret that he's still waiting for his money. I didn't mean to rip off him. I swear. The thing is that when I got back to Nairobi, things were, as they say, perilous! But I'm running ahead of my story . . ."

"It was as if Black Devil had smelled me return to the city. He turned up at the den almost immediately, carrying the previous day's newspaper.

" 'Look at this,' he said, opening the paper.

I saw my picture staring at me from the page. But it was the caption that very nearly made me pass out. It said: "Killer Carjacker Sought by Police." The Indian was offering a reward of fifty thousand shillings to anybody with information that would lead to my arrest and the recovery of the stolen car. A fortune seeker, I was about to become the source of somebody else's fortune!

"That's when I really saw Black Devil's—well—devilish side. He was ruthless. He accused me of going against his instructions and killing Sammy so that I could end up with his share of the money. He even swore he had a mind to give me a taste of my own medicine for treachery and betrayal."

"Sammy was dead?"

"That was news to me, but that's what the newspaper said," Ignatius said, sadly. "I gathered later that he never made it to the police station. His bullet-riddled body was found floating like a log in the Nairobi River a day after he was supposed to report the theft of his pickup to the police. The poor guy had rolled the dice and lost. What I found most alarming was that, according to the newspaper, *I* was the suspected murderer. I protested that I was no murderer," Ignatius went on, "but Black Devil merely smiled. 'Do you think the police will buy that?' he asked. 'Especially if they get to know of that other body you and your friends threw in the abandoned quarry?'

"Then, Black Devil looked at me coolly. I was in a fix, and he knew it. His devil's grin widened into an almost genuine smile. 'But we are friends. That's why I trusted you in the first place. If you have money, I'll help you settle matters with the police,' he said.

"I tried to explain what had happened in Kisumo, but Black Devil brushed me off irritably. 'Money talks,' he said icily. 'If you've got no money, I'm afraid there's nothing to be done. You'll have to carry your own cross. And from today, know this: YOU DON'T KNOW ME. WE'VE NEVER

MET AND YOU'VE NEVER EVEN HEARD MY NAME. UNDERSTAND?'

"I understood," Ignatius said, with a sigh. "I had been played, and there was nothing I could do. Fate had handed Black Devil a trump card, and I was at his mercy. The following week, he brought me out here. To get me out of reach of the police, he said. That, my friends, is how I sold my soul to the devil. And I've been in this forest ever since— for fifteen years!"

"Were you really at his mercy?" Mumbi asked. "You couldn't have gone to the police and told them what you knew?"

"Yeah, sure," Karoki agreed. "You had that choice, didn't you?"

"I'd still have ended up in jail for my part in the saga," Ignatius said. "I didn't want to go to jail. So, I chose what looked like the lesser evil, then."

"Well, choices have consequences," Karoki said. "Still, it's a real sad story."

"Yeah, real sad," Mumbi agreed. "If it's true," she added.

Ignatius grinned and turned towards the boys. "I told you about women—always so sceptical. But I swear that I tell the truth," he looked at the boys as if he expected some kind of response. "Well," he said after an interval. "I'm now at your mercy. You promised . . ."

"Yes, yes, of course, we promised," Mwenda interrupted. "But you'll have to help us get the Black Devil."

"He's dangerous! You've no idea what kind of beast he is," Ignatius said. "And he's invincible. The law seems to slip off his back like water. He can get away with everything. With *anything!*"

So then, the three of them—Mumbi, Karoki, and Mwenda—stepped aside to consult. They were no longer afraid that Ignatius would try to escape. After a while, they came back, and Karoki said, "If we're to deal with Black Devil, we must involve the police. We'll need your cooperation too, but you need not worry. All you need to do is to be honest. I believe the police will not mind making a deal if you help nail the drug baron."

"That will never work!" Ignatius cried.

"Why not?"

"The man has the police at his beck and call."

"Maybe he used to, but a lot of things have changed since last year. With the new government, there's a good chance that we can get him sent to jail," Karoki said.

"A new government?" Ignatius marvelled. "What happened to the old one?" he asked.

"Where have you been, man?" Mumbi laughed.

"In the underworld," Ignatius said, "I haven't left this forest in over a decade, you know."

"Well, then. BREAKING NEWS," Karoki said dramatically. "Yes, there's a new government. The old one was voted out of power."

"Good riddance!" Ignatius vehemently said.

Everybody except Mwenda laughed. "Let's go, guys," he called rather impatiently.

"You really mean to go ahead with this?" Ignatius asked.

"And why shouldn't we?" Mwenda retorted.

"The Black Devil—the man is vicious," Ignatius cried.

Mwenda tried to reassure the man. "Don't worry. At what time is he expected on the farm?"

"He always arrives as the sun goes down."

"Great," Mwenda said. "Let's get moving, guys."

"Alright," Ignatius said, reluctantly. "I'll show you the way."

"No, you are taking us right up to the plantations," Mwenda said.

"He'll hang me if he knows I took you to his farm!"

"No, he won't. We'll catch him before he gets you. We must rid our village of his menace at whatever cost. That's why we *must* get to the plantations before he arrives," Mwenda said. "We'll have an advantage if he finds us waiting for him."

Ignatius hesitated. For the first time, he seemed like he was looking to escape. Mwenda hefted his gun and said, "Do you need me to remind you of your options?"

"But you promised to let me go!"

"Yeah, on the condition you help us get Black Devil," Mwenda said. "You were to go—*after* you help us get the devil. That was the deal. Wasn't it?"

"I've been played, again!" Ignatius cried, throwing up his hands in the most despairing gesture that his fellow interlocutors had ever seen.

"No matter. Just play along and you'll be alright," Karoki said. "It's really about saving your skin, finally. Your hide or the devils? That's the question. If you want to carry his cross, well, that's your choice."

"Of course, if you do," Mwenda added, intensely fixing his gaze on Ignatius, "This mountain will be your Gethsemane. I promised, and I don't eat my words, ever. They give me indigestion, you know."

Mwenda sounded dead earnest. Looking at him, Ignatius was convinced that the boy meant every word he said. It finally dawned on Ignatius that the police who he had tried to elude all these years might be his only hope. The thought of it was unnerving, but resigned to his fate, Ignatius simply said, "Alright, brother."

"Good," Mwenda said. "That's the spirit."

Five

The chopper took off from a helipad atop Black Devil's house in the city at around four. The pilot was a tall, lean, aging man named Japheth. Flying Black Devil was a nerve-wracking job. He often had to land in far-flung places, deep in the jungle where Boss had interests, not only in growing drugs but also in poaching. As the small chopper took to the air, Japheth was in an unusually introspective mood.

Years ago, Japheth had been an airman with the Kenya Air force. He had been sacked in 1982, following the failed coup attempt. Still, he was luckier than most. The court martial handed him only a twelve-year jail term with hard labor. Japheth had always thought that he was a tough man, but the conditions at the Naivasha maximum security prison were humbling, to say the least. The place was as hot as hell and dusty, which for a soldier, was no great deal—but the labor! The daily digging and splitting of rocks was soul-sapping, even for a hardened soldier. Still, you had to admire the jailers. How they survived in this bleak, Godforsaken place was a miracle of human endurance. And they all seemed to have graduated with flying colors from hell's school of retribution. The kindest of the lot was a pitch-dark sergeant, a tough taskmaster who called himself Black Devil. The man bragged that he was licensed to kill. He had been known to crack a prisoner's skull with the butt of his rifle. And the prisoners were no better. To the everlasting amusement of the jailers, they fought worse than rabid dogs over the small rations of food.

When he finally came out of the prison, Japheth felt like he had just woken up from a nightmare. He had to keep pinching himself to make sure that he was indeed alive. But as he soon discovered, he had merely stepped from one chamber of hell into another. With his record, nobody was willing to give him a job. Everywhere he turned, the unspoken message was the same: *Once condemned, always condemned.* It was a heavy price to pay for the rashness of youth. Bitter and disillusioned, he took to drink—cheap, potent spirits that had a kick like a donkey's. Every time he went down, Japheth hoped that he would never rise up again. But every time, as if some malevolent god was mocking him, he somehow got back up on his feet again. His suffering was great. He was wondering when it would ever end when Pablo came to his rescue and offered him a job. It was an amorphous job. Japheth was going to be pilot, bodyguard, handyman, and everything else in-between. The job, as he soon discovered, had its rewards. Japheth embraced it with both hands. 'If they won't let you join them,' he said to himself, 'Beat them.'

But now, after years of working on the wrong side of the law and with a new regime in power, Japheth was beginning to have doubts. He wasn't sure how much longer their luck or more precisely—to hell with Pablo—*his* luck would hold. Once or twice, he had tactfully tried to broach the issue. Still, the Black Devil, as he had nicknamed *Pablo*, wouldn't even entertain the possibility that the regime might not take too kindly to his clandestine activities. Convinced that with money, no hurdle was too big for him to surmount,

Black Devil reacted with his usual, cocky self-assurance. He believed that everybody had a price and that money could buy him anything or anybody.

Still, Japheth feared that the devil was stretching their luck too far. Often, he thought about quitting. But he realized at once that quitting would not be easy. He knew too much about Black Devil and was afraid that he might walk out of a job and out of the world of the living. He wouldn't be the first down that route either. Needless to say, the prospect of death no longer seduced him as it once did. So, he bided his time and hoped for the best.

Now, as the rugged peaks of the mountaintop came into view, Japheth, like so many other times before, was exactly where he had started from: convinced that he needed to quit before it was too late but afraid of the consequences.

***

There was a distant drone in the sky. It came nearer and nearer as the chopper approached.

"That must be him, the Black Devil," Ignatius said. "He'll be here in a moment."

The words were hardly out of his mouth when the chopper appeared, flying so low that the forest shook. From their hiding place, Mwenda, Karoki, Ignatius, and Mumbi watched as it circled overhead like a huge iron bird.

"I've got a mind to shoot down the blasted thing," Mwenda said, excitedly.

"With an old, rusty gun? Karoki laughed. "That must pass as the joke of the year!"

"But why not? The Mau Mau . . ."

"Oh, you swallowed Ignatius's yarns about bringing down planes?"

"Aw, it's no myth," Ignatius protested. "The old man told me himself."

"Either way, I don't think it would be a good idea to shoot down the chopper even if you could," Mumbi said.

"I don't think so either," Karoki agreed.

After another round of the forest, the chopper appeared again. It approached into the wind, hovered over a clearing, and slowly landed. The gale from its rotating blades was so strong that it flogged the bush and forced all but the strongest of the trees to bow before the force. Around and beyond the clearing was Black Devil's expansive farm. Two men alighted and stood chatting outside the chopper. They looked relaxed, like they had just arrived for a picnic. Looking at them, it was obvious that trouble was the last thing on their minds. It seemed like they were waiting for somebody or something.

"That's Boss, the man in the white T-shirt," Ignatius said.

"Black Devil?"

"Yes," Ignatius said. "The other man is his handyman, Japheth. A real snitch too. Always bossing everybody around. I think they are waiting for us to go for the supplies."

"Us? What do you mean?"

"Us—the poor devils who work on the farm."

"How many of you are on the farm?"

"Five men on this farm . . . Twenty-five or so in all if you count the surrounding farms."

"And what kind of men are they?"

"Ruffians basically," Ignatius said. "Each of them has a colorful story of how he ended up here. But most of them are just hapless souls whose families lost everything during the Mau Mau war. They were squatters in the forest before the barons recruited them to work on the farms. The others are outlaws—fugitives—who, like me, ran away from the unforgiving city after falling afoul of the law."

"And they are all armed?"

"Yes, but mostly with machetes," Ignatius grinned, rather sheepishly. "The same we use to work on the farms with," he added.

"But you have guns, too?"

"Sure, but the men are not expecting any trouble. So, I don't think they'll be carrying guns," Ignatius said. "In any case, Black Devil would not trust anybody with a gun. Only his sidekick is allowed to be armed around him."

"Why? Is he paranoid or something?"

"I guess you might say that," Ignatius agreed. "But still, it's understandable, I think. If you're quick to do unto others what you wouldn't like them to do unto you, you won't be too comfortable with anybody holding a gun around you, either."

"And who is his sidekick?"

"Japheth, the pilot."

Mwenda still couldn't believe what he was hearing. In the village, it was said that the gangs in the forest farms were reckless outlaws, dangerously armed and quick on the trigger. Rumor had it that even the police dared not take on the gangs. Chief Mageca was always warning people not to dare to venture into the forest. Now, it seemed like these stories were exaggerated. Was the chief, who ought to know better, deliberately overplaying the viciousness of the gangs? If so, why? Or was Ignatius misleading them into some kind of trap?

"Are you sure?" Mwenda asked. "You know, if you try some monkey business . . ."

For an answer, Ignatius dabbed the ground with his finger, licked the tip of his finger, and pointing to the sky, he swore: "The sky-God is my witness!"

Then, Ignatius saw that Mwenda still didn't believe him. So, he explained: "In the beginning, when I first came here, there used to be a lot of violence. There were only a few farms, and pirates would steal our crop, so we had to be armed all of the time. That's no longer the case. The barons work well together, and the police don't bother us, so nowadays everything is rather easy and relaxed. If the barons sense some trouble, they might have us armed, but normally, there's not anything that cannot be settled with a machete."

Just then, five men emerged like shadows from the farm. They made a beeline for the aircraft, following each other in a single line through the lush green crop. Looking at the men, Karoki was pleasantly surprised. The sight of the men emboldened him. These were far from the vicious gangsters he had been led to expect. The men looked weather-beaten— pathetically so. Like some nocturnal creatures unexpectedly caught in the full light of day, they all looked a little dazed. And they didn't have any weapons—not even a single machete.

"I've got an idea!" Mumbi suddenly said as the men started to offload and carry away some cartons from the chopper. "What if Ignatius just takes me to him—the Black Devil, I mean?"

"I can't do that!" Ignatius cried. "The man is a rapist!" He added with self-righteous indignation.

"You were taking me just a while ago, weren't you?" Mumbi coolly said. "Anyway, listen: I'll pretend that I came willingly. That's sure to disarm him. Then you guys can move in."

Flustered, Karoki protested. "That's bold but a bit reckless, I'm afraid. There's something to be said about feminine wiles, to be sure, but I doubt you can pull it off with such a thug. And I don't think we want to take such a risk!"

"Besides," Mwenda added, "Can we really trust Ignatius when he's out of our reach? Suppose that he turns against us. That'll undo all that we have achieved. We'll end up looking like fools—even in our own eyes."

Ignatius was going to repeat his swearing ritual, but Karoki stopped him. Ignatius looked at Mwenda reproachfully and said: "You're the meanest guy I've met after Black Devil, my brother. How can I give her up to the tormentor after she stopped you from shooting me? If you had your way, I would be long dead by now."

"Most likely," said Mwenda, grinning.

"Alright, sister, let's go. Let's see if I'm the beast your brothers think I am," Ignatius said. It was clear that he was hurt that Mwenda still didn't trust him.

But they didn't go. Because just at that moment, an agonized cry followed by the *tut-tut-tut* of a gun rocked its way through the stillness of the forest. Looking, Mwenda and his team were met by the sight of an airborne man. Black Devil had been struck by a buffalo right next to his chopper!

Dancing on his shadow, the massive buffalo with horns and humps glistening in the sunlight, swiftly turned, and seemingly skimmed as if its feet didn't touch the ground. Then, the buffalo charged at the gunman who fled into the bush, running as if he had wings on his feet.

"Let's go. Quick, guys!" Mwenda said. "We must try and disarm him before he recovers his wits!"

"Yeah, but be careful," Ignatius warned. "The man is armed and dangerous."

"Don't worry, man," Mwenda said. "The Spirit is with us. I can feel it percussing in the wind!"

Skirting along the edge of the clearing and still keeping low, they came to where Japheth and the buffalo had crushed through the bush. Following the trail of blood, they found Japheth, shaken and gasping for breath, sitting just a few feet from where the wounded buffalo had collapsed in a heap. The scare had completely taken the wind out of his sails. But the buffalo wasn't yet done. Never one to say *die* and sensing that he was spent, the buffalo was determined not to go down alone. He somehow managed to rear his way back up. He sat first on his haunches and then, slowly climbed to his wobbly feet. Seeing the murderous glint in his eyes and knowing how absolutely wild a wounded buffalo could be, Ignatius shouted for boys to watch out and, on impulse, rushed to drag Japheth out of harm's way. Just then, the buffalo charged. It came crashing through the bush just as Ignatius pulled Japheth out of the way. He dug his horns into the spot where Japheth was supposed to be. When he reared his head, there was a mountain of soil across the bridge of his horns. Had Ignatius not been so swift, the buffalo would've impaled Japheth on the ground and left him to feed the forest hounds. But as it was, it was the buffalo that went down. He was felled as much by his mortal wounds as by the disappointment of failing to maim his prey. And this time, he never rose again.

"Thank you, mate," Japheth said, his voice shaking. "I think I've sprained my leg. Hurts like hell."

"Don't worry," Ignatius said in his most charming voice. "It will be attended to in a moment. I've got a nurse."

"A nurse?" Japheth asked, surprised.

"Yes, a nurse."

Ignatius heaved Japheth to his shoulders, and crawling on all fours like a prowling beast, lugged him into the bush where Mwenda, Karoki, and Mumbi were waiting.

But instead of a nurse, Japheth was met by a lad pointing at him with a gun.

"What's—?"

Ignatius clamped his mouth shut with his big paws. Karoki quickly disarmed him, and before Japheth realized what was happening, Mumbi dexterously blindfolded him with her own lesso.

Now with an additional gun, Mwenda and Karoki discussed their next plan of action. They decided that the best thing to do was to stay out of sight and wait. Ignatius agreed.

"I'm sure that my friends . . . eh, my *former* friends, will want to come and see what the buffalo has made of—" He twisted his mouth in a gesture to indicate Japheth. "At least, out of curiosity if for nothing else," he added.

They didn't wait long before the farmhands emerged from their quarters. Carrying knives and scrambling through the bush like hungry hounds, they gathered around the buffalo which was already in the throes of death. They were all real tramps—rustic and rather clownish. Listening to the men talk as they gleefully waited for the buffalo to die so that they could curve him carry away the meat, it was clear they had vastly more respect and sympathy for the buffalo than they had for Black Devil, who was painfully dragging himself back into the chopper. And they had a humor all their own—an earthy sense of humor that was as rugged and rustic as they were.

"The buffalo is a real fiend! Did you see how it tossed the Boss?" the oldest of the men said.

"Yeah, I thought the man had suddenly gotten himself a pair of wings."

"True . . . true . . . I thought he'd never come back to earth."

"I wish he had disappeared."

"Skywise to heaven, aye?"

"Heaven? They'd throw him right back, the devil!"

"A real fiend, this buffalo is!" the old man repeated. He still seemed awed by the bull which, even in his final death throes, wore its scowl like a badge of honor.

"You'd be a fiend too if somebody castrated you and cut off your tail!"

"Aw, what kind of a joke is that, man?" somebody sniggered.

"Joke? Who's joking now? Look, somebody tore off his balls."

"Yeah, sure! God, that must have been P-A-I-N-F-U-L. I dare not imagine!"

"That's the hyenas' idea of humor."

"Macabre humor!"

The buffalo had a big raw wound where his balls should have been. As the men talked, it transpired that incidences of hyenas biting off buffalo testicles and tails were on the rise in the forest. The hyenas, the men, said, mostly targeted calves and must have picked on the bull because he was an old loner.

"You can't blame the hyena," the old man said. "He was used to scavenging on what the lion left behind, so what did you expect him to do after you killed off almost all the lions?"

"I guess he had to learn new tricks."

"Yes, and how better to learn than by picking the low-lying fruits to begin with—tails and balls!"

"Still, that must have been one bold hyena!"

"Sure, but you know the hyena. If it's your balls he wants, he'll get them. He's ever so persistent."

The men laughed. Already, the feisty buffalo's fate was sealed. A kettle of vultures was wheeling above and gathering in the trees, patiently waiting to clear off what remained of the buffalo once the men were done with it. It was unnerving to think of the fate that awaited the beast, which only a moment ago had stormed through the bush like a war tank.

"Japheth managed to get away?"

"Yeah. I bet you he's still running. Somebody should tell him that the buffalo is dead."

"I'll send him a telegram. He must be in Karatina town by now."

The men laughed again. Karoki almost laughed too. *Didn't the men know that the telegram went off in the way of the Dodo, eons ago?* he wondered.

He decided to silence the clowns. Aiming just above their heads, Karoki fired. It was just as he had expected. The men went down as the bullet wheezed over their heads, buzzing like a wasp. In a perfectly choreographed move, he and Mwenda burst forth, with their guns at the ready. *Just like in the movies*, Karoki thought.

"Lie low like antelopes!" Mwenda ordered the men.

"What's the joke, boy?" The old man asked.

"Joke?" Mwenda sniggered. "You're under arrest!"

"Why would good boys want to arrest their grandfather?"

"Boys?" Karoki retorted. "Well, maybe you missed the memo, but I've got news for you, old man. We are men— total men. The *baddest* men you've ever met, Papa."

The old man looked amused. "Alright," he said after an interval. "Why should you want to arrest me, pray?"

"Well, for murder, drug trafficking, poaching. You know the gig, don't you? Lots of mean and dirty crimes," Mwenda replied.

"I'll tell you what," the old man said, very calmly. "Why don't you go for the big man?"

"Black Devil?"

"Yes—the same! He's up there in his plane, sore as a boil. Just had a jig with the buffalo."

"Don't worry," Mwenda said. "We'll pay him a courtesy call in a while. Now lie low, Papa, and stop blabbering."

The boys quickly dispossessed the workers of their knives and led the men into the bush. Upon arrival, they couldn't hide their surprise at seeing Ignatius with a girl. The girl was supposed to be in Black Devil's bunker, not here in the bush. Surprise quickly turned into bewilderment when they recognized the blindfolded man.

"Japheth? What's going on?" One of the men asked.

"Oh, nothing," Ignatius quickly said. "These lads just decided to throw a party."

"Party, hell!" Japheth said. He was seething with rage. "You're a despicable traitor—so double-faced, Ignatius!" He blurted out.

"Aren't we all?" Ignatius retorted. "Anyway, welcome to the party, brothers. The more the merrier!"

Only one of the men had a belt. Mwenda ordered Papa to take a machete. Ignatius readily gave him his machete, and Mwenda briskly shepherded the old man into the bush. A short while later, when they returned, Papa was carrying straps of the wattle bark. The boys used the ropes to tie up the men, trussing up their hands. Japheth tried to resist when the boys tied him. He was so stunned when Ignatius struck him that after that, he gave no more trouble. The boys tied him up. Ignatius was impressed by the boys' resourcefulness.

"You're doing fine," he said.

"Very fine indeed!" Mumbi echoed. She could barely believe that these were the same boys she knew. Something seemed to have come over them—a single-mindedness that was both thorough and a little frightening.

"Now for the final and biggest tackle of all," Mwenda said. "The devil—no less!"

Mumbi solemnly crossed herself. Her lips moved as she said a silent prayer. She determinedly tightened the lesso around herself, and the four of them set off toward the chopper. They could hear Black Devil groaning like an old tractor as they approached the chopper. It appeared the buffalo had badly wounded him.

The chopper's seats were arranged for five passengers, facing each other in configuration. Keeping low behind Ignatius and Mumbi, the two boys crept up behind the seat. Black Devil was sprawled across the seat that faced to the front of the chopper. His T-shirt was torn and drenched in the blood where the buffalo had jabbed him just below the ribs.

"Oh, good gracious!" Ignatius exclaimed. "What happened, Boss?"

"A buffalo . . ." Black Devil groaned. "It . . . nearly . . . nearly killed me, Ignatius."

He saw Mumbi, and a little light seemed to come into his eyes. "Oh, what a beautiful damsel you have, today . . ."

"I was in luck, Boss."

"On my unluckiest day?" Black Devil said grumpily. His voice tapered almost to a whisper, "I'm done . . . Ignatius . . . Done! I'm no good for anything—nothing at all," he grumbled. "That buffalo . . . I don't know what Japheth was doing. He didn't see the demon coming . . . Or maybe he did. I think he wanted the buffalo to kill me. Oh, my God . . . But I'll deal with him. It's about time I got another guard too."

"Don't worry, Boss. I've taken care of the buffalo. It'll never bother you again," Ignatius said. "And from now on, *we'll* take care of you."

"You'll take care of me?"

"Yes, sir," Mumbi said. "I'll nurse your wounds. Would you like me to take care of your wounds?" She smiled, bright as the sun.

"Of course . . . Of course," Black Devil said. He sounded as though he was already beginning to feel better.

Mumbi went over and examined his wounds. It looked like somebody had stuck and twisted a dagger into him where the buffalo's horns had torn into his body. It was a wonder that the buffalo hadn't ripped his guts out. Mumbi started to clean the wounds with her lesso.

"You said you killed the buffalo, Ignatius?"

"Yes, Boss," Ignatius replied with a straight face.

"Good!" Black Devil said. "That's why I like you, Ignatius. You're so dependable. Japheth: I don't know what grew where his brain was supposed to be. He doesn't think much. Maybe he has a tumor in the brain. I hope it's a tumor, anyway. In any case, I've long suspected that he was planning on quitting. But I'll deal with him. I'll make an example of him. Nobody crosses me and gets away with it—never, ever."

He seemed to be weighing something in his mind. After a while, he went on, "Now do this. Go get the buffalo's . . . Okay, I don't want to speak that in front of a lady, but you know what I mean. Don't you?"

"Yes. You mean I get his balls?" Ignatius said with a chuckle.

"You really are uncouth!" Black Devil laughed. "But now that you've said it, yes. You know, the Chinese swear by the rhino's horn. They say it's a good aphrodisiac. We humor them, of course, and give them what they want. But they've got no idea. Nothing beats the buffalo's you-know-what for an aphrodisiac. And that's just what I need right now. Well roasted and seasoned with herbs. It's a magical prescription for health, strength, and virility. Our forefathers discovered that a long time ago. Hurry now, man, before the hyenas and the vultures beat us to it."

"The hyenas already did, Boss," Ignatius said.

"Heck! They did?"

"Yes. Long before the buffalo was dead."

"I don't know what's wrong with the hyenas in this forest," Black Devil grumbled.

"They suddenly seem to have taken up some very bad manners."

Suddenly, Mwenda and Karoki popped up from behind the seats. Both their guns were drawn.

"They are in good company, it seems," Karoki said.

"The hyenas used to feed on the lions' kill," Mwenda added. "What did you expect them to do after you and you and your friends got rid of most of the lions?" Mwenda demanded. "The hyenas had to learn to look for they own food, yeah?"

"But your game is up!" Karoki said.

Black Devil turned to Ignatius, a quizzical expression on his face.

"Meet our new bosses, Boss," Ignatius grinned.

"What do you mean? Somebody is trying to take over my farm?"

"Not trying, Boss," Ignatius replied, "They've already taken it over."

"As a matter of fact, you're under arrest!" Mwenda said.

"What!" Black Devil tried to sit up.

"You heard me right," Mwenda said. "And don't move or—"

Black Devil crumbled back on the seat. He looked slightly amused, as though he still couldn't believe his eyes or his ears. It was as though he thought this was nothing but a foolish, boyish prank. As though he expected that the boys would soon come to their senses and everything would turn out to be what he thought it was: a recklessly stupid joke.

"What's going on, Ignatius?" he asked.

"Exactly what you see here, Boss. We're outmaneuvered. Everybody on the farm has been arrested, and there's nothing that can be done about it, no."

"The police are here?"

"We're the police," Mwenda said.

"Well, the police have always been my friends. I'm sure that we can talk," Black Devil smiled. The smile looked more like a snarl. It parted his lips but didn't reach his shifty eyes.

"Yes, sure," Mwenda said. "But be warned, I don't like people trying to play monkey business with me. I really don't."

"Nobody needs to fool around," Black Devil said. "I certainly have no time for pranks. I'm sure we'll come to some understanding."

"Good. So, let's start from the beginning," Karoki said. "Once upon a time, there was a man named Sammy Onyango. He used to be a driver for a certain Indian in Nairobi. You remember the dude? Maybe you can start by telling us about what *really* happened to him?"

"Yeah, man," Mwenda said. "The police thought Ignatius killed him, but our investigations seem to tell a different story."

"What nonsense you speak!" Black Devil exploded. He seemed to realize his mistake immediately and though a little patronizing, he was more reconciliatory when he said, "You know, it's unbecoming to disturb the dead. Who knows, but his spirit might return to haunt you."

"Well, speaking for myself, I'm not scared of any spirits," Mwenda said with a chuckle. "I believe in a more resurgent spirit: the spirit of the Rainbow Dragon! Ever heard of it?"

"Nope," Black Devil curtly said. "Is it Chinese?"

"Nope," Mwenda retorted. "It's the spirit of those who straighten up things. Too bad you don't know how to listen; otherwise, you'd have heard it in the wind all over the forest. If only you knew how to listen, you'd have heard it in the songs of the birds. You'd have heard it telling you that one day, it will catch up with you," Mwenda said.

Just then, Karoki remembered Ignatius's story about the old man of Mwisho wa Reli, and something clicked in his mind.

"It is the spirit of the fearless ones," he said excitedly. "The daring ones who bring down enemy planes with a machete!"

Ignatius suddenly slapped himself in the face—*clap, clap, clap*—and exclaimed: "The ones who bring down enemy planes! How come I never thought about it that way? How come I never thought about the spirit of those brave men?" he cried.

"Well, I think you said it yourself," Karoki murmured. "It's because you sold your soul to the devil. So, you could never really understand the spirit of the stories that the old man was telling you. You always thought he was a fabulist. You thought his stories were only stories—the wild fantasies of some cracked old man," Karoki said. "But I don't blame you," he added. "I didn't understand when you told us the story either, but now I do."

Black Devil seemed overwhelmed and a bit amused by all the strange talk. He turned to Ignatius and demanded: "Since when did you become friends with these crazy tots?"

"Well, they arrested me over Sammy's death," Ignatius said. "You remember him, don't you? You remember the police placed a prize on my head?"

"But that was such a long time ago!"

"Yes, a long time ago, but it seems the dude is reaching out from the grave to haunt us," Ignatius said.

"You're right he is," Karoki said. "In any event, murder cases remain open in perpetuity or until the crime is resolved. You never get away with murder. If you don't answer for the crime on this side of heaven, you'll surely answer on Judgment Day. But we're keen—very keen—that whoever killed the poor fellow should face the consequences of his crime here and NOW, in this life. So, we've been investigating. Besides, the prize must now have increased substantially if you add up the interest. That's quite an appetizer. Isn't it?"

"Oh, so it's money you want?" Black Devil asked. He sounded relieved. "Well," he went on without waiting for an answer, "I may give you money but don't think that you can blackmail me. Nobody tries that with me."

"Nobody?" Mwenda retorted. "Well, that's because you hadn't met us."

As the boys led him away at gunpoint, Black Devil was too stunned to say anything. When he finally found his voice, he was nearly berserk with fury. He accused Ignatius of betrayal and threatened the boys.

"I assure you you'll regret this," he said. "I swear I'll slice you up with my own hands; so fine that by the time that I'm through with you, there won't be anything left for even the maggots to feed on. Nobody ever crosses me and gets away with it!"

"Yeah, sure," Karoki sneered. "They end up in the river, dead!"

Six

As dusk fell, alarm swept through Hombe village like a whirlwind. Three youths—Aileen Mumbi, Pius Mwenda, and grandmother Rakeli's grandson, Stephen Karoki—were missing. Grandmother Rakeli was beside herself with worry. The elders sent to the chief. His wife said he had gone to the County Headquarters. He had not returned home by evening, and when the sun started to go down, Grandmother declared that she would go to the forest herself and find the children. The women calmed her down, but afterward, she wouldn't eat or drink. The villagers gathered at her home. It was then that the elders decided to take matters into their own hands and send a search party into the forest. They lit a big bonfire in Grandmother's compound and kept vigil, awaiting the group's return.

The search was led by a burly young man of twenty-five named Kiongo. He seemed surprised when the elders picked him. But the elders had their reasons. Kiongo knew the forest better than any other young man. He was always getting into trouble with the chief for defying his orders against venturing to the forest. But whenever the chief confronted him, Kiongo said he went to the forest only to listen to the song of the forest and to hear what the birds were saying. It was a weird excuse for his intractability. Nobody else seemed to have heard this song. The chief was convinced that the young man was up to no good.

As he said to anybody who would listen, "The man was likely to be one of the criminals who regularly harassed the villagers in the forest. It's either that or he's taking drugs. But you just wait," the chief would say, "The long arm of the law is not disabled. One of these fine days, it will catch up with the miscreant!"

But Kiongo would not be intimidated. For the longest time, he had been spying on the forest gangs, and whenever he heard about the chief's threats, he would say, "It's true that the law has a long arm. But why doesn't the chief, who has police officers at his beck and call, not first arrest the forest criminals? Why, if he thinks I'm a criminal, doesn't he just go ahead and arrest me?" Then without waiting for an answer, he would say to whoever he was speaking to: "*Tafakari hayo.*"

And people thought but no matter how hard anybody thought about it, they couldn't come up with a satisfactory answer. But Kiongo thought he already knew the answer. And so, after overcoming his initial surprise, he jumped at the opportunity to lead the search with unusual zeal.

Meanwhile, in Grandmother's wattle and daub house, where she would not be persuaded to take even a cup of tea, all the women pined and prayed for the lost children.

Around the fire, the elders kept their apprehension to themselves, hiding their fear behind a wide-ranging banter, which touched on anything and everything except the reason for their unusual gathering. In the manner of the old, they talked about the good old days before the white men came along and ruined everything. With their voices taut with filial pride, they talked about the gallant sons of the village: fighters who would bring down white planes with guns that they had fashioned with their own hands; legends who could throw a machete for seven miles and right on target. These were real straighteners smoothing their ways into a brighter future, watering the tree of freedom with their blood.

The elders talked of dreams realized and the festering wounds of dreams long deferred. They talked late into the night, but when a chilly breeze blew down from the mountain and whispered in the trees, the men worried about the lost children. *Why was the search team taking so long to return?*

One murmured, "Let's pray they didn't stray into the farms and into trouble."

"But why would they go that far?"

"Well, I wouldn't be surprised. That boy, Mwenda, he's always courting trouble. He must have enticed the others to go into the forest in the first place. You remember the bomb?"

"Yes. I'm afraid it isn't beyond him to go all the way into the farms."

"You know his grandfather died in the forest. Maybe it's his spirit that calls the boy there. Who knows?"

"Well, it's surely a bad omen when the spirit of the dead calls you, but I don't think old Mwenda died in the forest. I've heard it said that he was among a band of fighters led by General Mathenge. They all managed to escape when the British bombed their bases in the forest. When politicians started to negotiate with the colonialists, the General was so piqued that with some die-hard fighters, he fled to Ethiopia, promising to return when the time was ripe to finish off the aborted war."

"And you believe that? Well, I don't," another said. "I mean, even if it's true that they somehow managed to escape, they must be very old men by now. That's supposing that they are still alive in the first place. If they ever come back at all, it would be to die at home, not to fight. Only young men fight wars!"

"That's true. Still, there's no denying that Mwenda has his grandfather's restless spirit."

"Well, aren't all boys naturally restless?"

"I suppose they are. Restless and reckless too, like the young, inexperienced bull that mounts the cow from the front and gets gored between the legs. What I don't understand is how your daughter got caught up in the matter, Ng'ang'a?"

"Oh, I don't, either," Mumbi's father said. "It's quite unlike her to play truant."

"Or is it that city boy? You know, we could all be sitting here worrying, and maybe the lads aren't in the forest, after all."

Ng'ang'a bristled at the insinuation that his daughter might have run off with the boy from the city, but he simply said, "You never know with children, these days."

And so, the men of the village talked. And in another corner of the compound, the youths of the village, in the shadows and out of earshot, speculated on what could have happened to their friends.

"I don't think there's much to the whole thing," a sixteen-year-old boy named Kamuto declared.

"How come?" somebody else demanded.

"I suspect that the city boy, Karoki, eloped with Mumbi," Kamuto opined.

"Then what about Mwenda? Two men cannot possibly abscond with one girl!" somebody observed.

"Don't be daft!" Kamuto retorted. "Karoki and Mwenda are the best of friends. I think they made a deal. Mwenda was to persuade Mumbi to go to the city with Karoki, and in return, Karoki was going to take Mwenda to the city with him. You'll never see Mwenda in this village again!"

"Yes, it is not beyond him to fix such a deal. He's quite mischievous, you know."

"But what about school?"

"Aw, school nothing! Mwenda would not even think twice about giving it a pass if he knew how."

"But there's still one thing you guys are forgetting," Njema inveighed.

"What?" Kamuto demanded.

"Mumbi is not that type of a girl," Njema said. "Besides, she is a woman. Karoki is still just a boy. So, far as I can see, the two can't tango."

The other boys laughed at this, and the debate continued on for a while. Then, the boys started to talk about other things. Why did it appear as if there were human images on the moon? No, those were not human images. They were footprints left behind by the first people to land on the moon. The boys argued about whether it was the Russians or the Americans who had first landed on the moon. Most of the boys argued that it was the Americans. The argument came to an inconclusive end when, just past midnight, the search team returned. Kiongo reported that they had gone as far as they could into the forest, but they still hadn't found the youths. The elders ruled that the search must resume in the morning.

***

Meanwhile, in the forest, Mwenda, Mumbi, and Karoki rounded up their captives. It was getting late now, and they needed to find a place to spend the night. Ignatius suggested they should spend the night in the workers' quarters, but Mwenda, still suspicious of the man, was not so sure. To him, it did not seem beyond Ignatius to set them up. And with the quarters so deep in the forest and so close to the adjacent farms, Mwenda feared that if something were to go wrong in the night, they would be at the mercy of the attackers.

Ignatius shrugged resignedly. The only other alternative he could think of was Black Devil's bunker down by the river. But knowing the Boss, Ignatius was mortally afraid that if Black Devil was somehow to extricate himself from the dire situation he was in, which Ignatius did not rule out, the devil would never forgive him for taking the intruders to the secret heart of his operations.

"Well," Mwenda said. "I think we had better go back to the Mau Mau caves."

"Then we had better hurry before the night stalkers begin to prowl," Mumbi said.

"Night stalkers?" Karoki gasped.

"Yes. Leopards, lions, hyenas," Mumbi said with a chuckle.

"There are pretty few lions in the forest these days," Ignatius said. "As for the others? Well, those are easy to handle. In any case, it's still too early for them to be out. But we need to pass by the workers' quarters all the same."

"Why do we *need* to?" Mwenda demanded.

Ignatius flashed his naughty, sheepish grin. "I need to collect something," he said.

"No monkey business?"

"Swear!" Ignatius said, laughing.

The workers' huts looked desolate in the gathering dusk. Some still had the doors wide open, just the way the workers had left them when they rushed out to see the buffalo. Ignatius went into the first hut. Papa demurred, wanting to know what Ignatius was going to do in his house. Ignatius just grinned. He did not say a word. Shortly thereafter, the angry squawks of a hen shattered the quiet evening. When

Ignatius emerged a moment later, he was carrying a big cock under his arm.

"What do you want with my cock?" Papa demanded.

Just then, he saw a packet of maize flour sticking from the pocket of Ignatius's jungle jacket.

"And my flour!" Papa cried. "The thieving monkey is stealing my ration of flour!" The old man protested.

"Calm down, Papa. You won't be needing any rations anymore," Ignatius coolly said. "The way things stand, we might as well have our Last Super in the forest tonight."

"Yeah," Japheth spat in disgust. "Before you get us all jailed or hanged," he darkly added.

Impressed by Ignatius's ingenuity and foresight, Mwenda, Karoki, and Mumbi could not stop laughing. They had been too preoccupied to think about food. But now, with the promise of a sumptuous meal of *ugali* and chicken in the air, they all suddenly felt very hungry.

"He's such an intelligent man," Karoki said in admiration.

"Ignatius?" Mumbi asked between bursts of mirth.

"Yes," Karoki replied.

"He is," Mumbi agreed. "It's such a shame that he allowed himself to get mixed up with all these cold-hearted fellows."

After a long march through the jungle, Mwenda, Karoki, and Mumbi brought their prisoners to the Mau Mau caves. Mumbi was jittery about spending the night in the caves. Mwenda made her even more apprehensive when he started to tell her about the skeleton along the wall of the cave. She wouldn't even let Mwenda show her the skeleton—especially after he said he believed it belonged to his grandfather, who had disappeared all those many years ago.

"Why don't we go back to the village?" she said.

"It's a long way to the village from here," Mwenda said. "But we can still try to make it if you don't mind risking a tango with one of your night stalkers!"

"Oh!" Mumbi cried.

They fetched firewood and lit a fire to keep themselves warm and to scare away the wild animals. An inner chamber of the cave was assigned to Mumbi. Ignatius and the boys would share the outer chamber with their prisoners, taking turns to watch over them. Ignatius immediately went to work, preparing super. To distract their minds from the hunger which gnawed at their stomachs like rats, the three friends ordered their prisoners to tell them their stories. They didn't expect anyone to have nearly as colorful a story as Ignatius's. However, they were in for a surprise.

"What's your name, mister?" Mumbi asked one of the delinquents.

"Ngethe. Onesmus Ngethe," he said.

"Okay, Ngethe, tell us your story," Mumbi directed.

"Oh, no, madam, please," Ngethe protested. "I am no storyteller!"

"Just try," Mwenda said to the man, "A man should do at least one good thing in his life before he dies."

"I've done lots of good in my life, but what good has it done me?" Ngethe complained. "Besides, I've already been dead once, so don't think you can scare me, talking about death."

The boys all laughed. Ngethe was another crank.

"Well, you can laugh," Ngethe said bitterly, "but don't forget that I was once as young as you are and full of dreams."

His discomforting words were followed by silence. His listeners were a bit embarrassed and didn't know what to say.

"Then what happened?" Karoki asked after a while. There was a tinge of something like sympathy in his voice.

"Well, I died. That's all."

"Died?" Mumbi, Mwenda, and Karoki exclaimed in unison. They wondered if they were dealing with a ghost. Seeing their perplexed reaction, the goons laughed. Apparently, they all knew Ngethe's story.

"Yes, *died*," Ngethe said, almost fiercely. "But my descent into the pits started as soon as I came out from the University of Nairobi . . ."

Ngethe paused when he noticed the look of disbelief on his young listeners' faces. He was not surprised. Sometimes, when he thought about his life, he too could not believe that he had ever set foot in a classroom, let alone a university lecture hall.

"I know I don't look the part, but I'm actually a graduate. An engineer in fact," he said with a smile. "My life took a downward turn sometime in the 1990s. There were agitators all over the place, calling for the expansion of the democratic space. Times were hard. The economy was in the doldrums. I was working, but what I earned was hardly enough to cover my nakedness—yes, it was that bad. But there was also a lot of money going around in certain circles. One of my friends from University had already gotten into politics and was doing quite well. One day, I met him. He told me how dumb it was for me to continue toiling as a government engineer. He suggested that I start my own business. If I was interested, he said we could work together. He promised to show me where fortunes were being made. My friend wanted me to start a company. He would look for the jobs and channel them to my company for a share of the proceeds. He talked about astronomical profits. I trusted him. You see, he had always been a religious man, and now that he had some power, I thought he ought to know what he was talking about. That proved to be my undoing."

"How was that?"

"To begin with, I did not have money to set up a company. I couldn't possibly ask my friend for the money, of course, for though poor, I was a proud man. So, I took the only option I had. I turned to my father. I asked him to allow me to use the title of our family land as collateral for a loan with the bank. That's when I learned what an emotional attachment my father had to the land. After days and long lectures from my father about how people had fought and shed blood for the land, he agreed to my request, staking his everything on me. Soon, my company—Goldwise Engineering and Consultants Inc (my friend suggested the name)—was up and running. I was the Managing Director, the Chief Engineer, the Secretary, Clerk, and Messenger. I did not have a coin to spare, but my friend said that it was okay. Faith is the substance of things hoped for, he said. The evidence of things not seen. I believed him."

"My friend knew what he was doing. For soon afterward, I clinched some tenders. My pall made sure the jobs kept coming. They were small at first, but as time went by, they got progressively bigger and bigger. Soon we were dealing in gold. We made quite a tidy heap of hay. The icing on the cake—is that the expression?—was that everything was tax-free. My friend said only halfwits pay tax. And so, the company grew, and with it came money and power. Wherever I went, doors opened before me. I became a very astute operator in the world of money and power games. That was to be expected. I had the shrewdest Godfather in town. That's until he contrived to deprive me of my company."

Ngethe paused. His expression went through the gamut of contortions before a weary smile settled on his face. Outside the cave, the hyenas and hounds were doing what they did best. They laughed and howled into the night. An owl hooted as well, somewhere not too far away. Ignatius glanced at Black Devil and turned away, a knowing smile playing on his lips.

"What's it?" Mumbi asked him.

"The owl . . ." Ignatius grinned, "You know: they say that when the owl hoots, someone is dying or about to die."

"That's nonsense. Don't count on it," Mumbi admonished. She turned to Ngethe and asked him to continue with his story.

"You've got to give it to him. My benefactor is a genius," Ngethe mused. It was almost as if he was speaking to himself. "An evil genius!" He added.

"He's still around?" Karoki asked.

"What a question!" Ngethe exclaimed. "Yes, he's still around. He's a Minister. One day, somebody should really look into how the fellow managed to reinvent himself and manoeuvre his way into the new government. But as I say, the guy is a genius. The ultimate conman. That, anyhow, is how he edged me out of the company. I didn't see it coming. Even to this day, I still marvel at how easily—how swiftly—it happened."

"Tell us about that?"

"It was easy—too easy. My friend simply unleashed the hounds on me. Suddenly, the tax authorities were on me. Everywhere I turned, there was one of those geeks. They came by day and by night, demanding this and that and talking about obscene penalties. Meanwhile, my friend had disappeared into thin air. I used to think I had many friends, but it's only when you're in real trouble that you realize how fickle friendship is. All my friends had disappeared. I was a marked man, and none of them would touch me with a one-mile pole. It was as if I had become some kind of contagious vermin. Suddenly, I was a man alone against a hostile world.

Before I knew it, I was in court. I jumped bail and made a dash for it. Too fast, I think, for somewhere on the way to Namanga, I had a grisly accident. I died on the spot. That's the way it is with misfortune. When it falls in love with you, it comes in bevies."

"Heck, so what are you? A ghost?" Karoki said.

"Yes, that doesn't make sense at all," Mumbi said. "You imagine you can scare us? The only person I know who ever resurrected was Jesus Christ, but then he was God!"

"The police took my body to the House of the Dead," Ngethe went on, ignoring the interruption. "My father disowned me in death. A few of my buddies organized a simple and quick funeral at a public cemetery. I guess they wanted to get me done with and forgotten. Anyway, on the day they were to bury me, a most strange thing happened. I was lying in the casket, very dead, like the dead always are. Then, a strange feeling got hold of me. I was lifting out of my body! As though from a perch high up, I saw my body lying there in that casket and a small group of mourners surrounding it, singing send-off hymns . . .

"I don't know how to explain the whole experience. My soul was floating over the gathered mourners, watching everything. I even saw some of my estranged friends, all suitably dressed in sombre dark suits. Somebody was making a speech. He said what an enterprising fellow I had been and how I had left such a deep void in the world of business and in their souls. You know the script, don't you? Speaking on behalf of my friends, he said how they would always treasure the memory of our times together . . . how I'd always live on in their hearts. Then something unusual: my soul descended and entered my body! I tried to sit up, but I was too squeezed-up in that coffin.

Then, I heard somebody say, "The casket moves!"

I recognized the voice. It belonged to one of my bosom friends. So, I called out, 'Let me out, Japheth!'

". . . He is here, so he can confirm what I say is true."

The three youths looked at the storyteller questioningly. Without uttering another word, Ngethe pointed at the pilot. The three youths could not hide their surprise at this twist in the story. They stared at Japheth quizzically. Their eyes asked: *Is it true?*

"It is true," Japheth said. "By the time I let him out of the coffin, everyone else had fled. I took him to town and bought him some food and lots of beer to welcome him back to the world of the living . . ."

Ngethe sighed. "That was nothing compared to what I saw when I went back to the village to see my folks. The whole village declared me a ghost and fled. I was banned from ever setting foot there!" Ngethe said, "I had no choice but to go back to the city."

"I found him a job," Japheth interjected.

"But you never told me I was hiring a ghost!" Black Devil glared. He turned to Ngethe, "You are here and now fired! I want nothing to do with ghosts. They are a bad omen."

Ngethe said, "Don't work yourself up, Boss. I don't think you're in a position to sack anyone, right now."

"But the whole story sounds incredible. I just don't believe one bit of it," Karoki declared.

"In actual fact, I don't think Ngethe was dead," Japheth said. "The whole thing is what we call a near-death experience. When I worked in the armed forces, we used to hear a lot from battlefronts about those kinds of experiences. They involve a situation in which the soul leaves the body, usually after a major trauma such as an accident. They are, however, very rare. Not everyone who is near death has this experience," Japheth explained knowledgeably.

"You are a soldier, then?" Karoki asked Japheth.

"I was," Japheth said, simply.

Black Devil's empire was indeed a web of evil run by some very queer characters, Karoki thought. He was sure there must be an interesting story behind the pilot, but he was tired and hungry, and Ignatius was getting ready to share the food. Besides, a man who dies and comes back to life was just too much for one night.

Seven

The following morning, as the crimson rays of dawn shot through the treetops, Mumbi, Mwenda, and Karoki made sure that their prisoners were still properly bound. Black Devil complained about his wounds. Ignatius went out. He returned shortly with some herbs. Mumbi helped him clean the wounds, and Ignatius treated them with the herbs. Karoki marvelled at the sure and confident way in which Ignatius went about the job.

"I learned quite a bit from that Samburu medicine man back in Mwisho," Ignatius said. "Besides, after all those years in the forest, we rarely had any other medicine except herbs. So, I guess I'm quite good at it," he added.

Then, they secured the entrance to the cave with huge rocks. They had agreed that Mwenda would remain behind, guarding the cave, while Mumbi and Karoki would go and explore Black Devil's farm. Ignatius was going to be the guide. When they left, Mwenda sat outside the cave, munching on some wild fruits. The sword leaned on the rock beside him and the gun stayed on his lap.

Ignatius led the way. He knew the forest intimately, and he showed his companions various shortcuts. The morning air was as chaste as a bride. The ancient trees looked regal in the soft light of morning. Walking underneath the trees, the three followed the meandering curve of the river. Along the way, they picked fruits, some unknown, which Ignatius said were good to eat. Everything was so fresh—so serene. The birds were singing in the trees. They were full of joy as if for them, Christmas had arrived early. This, Karoki thought, munching on a luscious red fruit, must be what God meant the world to be when on creation day, He looked at His work and declared it good.

At long last, they arrived at their destination. Karoki saw the bhang farms now in the full light of morning. He was outraged by the sheer scale of the destruction visited on the tranquil forest, a massive chunk of which had been cleared to make way for the farms. Not even the sacred Migumo trees had been spared. Water had been diverted from the river to supply the farms. Around the workers' camp, little gardens shimmered with the most succulent vegetables that Karoki had ever seen. Hens wallowed in the dust. *Probably wondering what became of Mr Cock,* Karoki thought. He and Mumbi gawked in amazement at the expansive farms. None of them had ever seen marijuana before. It was difficult to comprehend how any person in his right senses could grow such a drug on such a large scale.

Ignatius saw their astonishment and smiled warily, "There are more farms beyond the river. Want to see?"

He led the two youngsters to an elevation along the edge of the farm, where a watchtower had been constructed. They climbed up a ladder and from the tower, looking over the forest breakers that demarcated the farms, they saw across the river endless green hills rolling with the crop. It was like being in the middle of the sprawling tea plantations of Kericho, Karoki thought. His heart plummeted when he thought about the barons who ran the farms. They must be very powerful to get away with this kind of destructive business. Had he and his friends taken up an impossible mission?

"How do they get away with this?" Mumbi asked.

"Money works miracles in this country," Ignatius said, simply. "And Black Devil . . . that brute can buy anything he wants, including the allegiance and protection of any office. You know, what he didn't tell you is that works with Ngethe's former Godfather. The two make a formidable team, I tell you."

Ignatius led his friends down to the river at the bottom of the valley. Upstream, the river suddenly dipped down into a small fall, around five metres high. Ignatius stood along the base of the fall with the water splashing over his body.

"I have a surprise for you," he said.

Then—wonder of wonders—Ignatius opened a heavy steel door that was embedded in the slope of the fall. "You can come in," he said, disappearing into the cave.

"What a cave!" Karoki cried when he entered.

Opening into a narrow tunnel and reinforced all around with stone and cement, the cave, though narrow at the entrance, gradually widened into a corridor that led to a storehouse. Ignatius found a solar lamp in the store, and switching it on, said, "If you want evidence of Ngethe's genius, look no further than this. He designed and constructed this bunker for Black Devil."

"He must have been inspired by the Mau Mau caves?"

"Obviously!" Mumbi said, coming up behind him.

The bunker was full of supplies, including everything one would need to survive in the forest. Karoki helped himself to some biscuits and passed some to Mumbi, who was busy looking at herself in a mirror.

"I need to freshen up," she said. "Might there by any chance be a bathroom, toiletries?"

Ignatius laughed. "We wash in the river," he said. "But yes, there's soap. Come, let me show you."

When he came back, Ignatius shook his head and said: "Girls. They'd rather bathe than eat if that was the choice."

Mumbi did not take long. When she came back, she was as bright as Christmas morning, smelling sweet and fresh.

"Unfortunately, we don't have dresses here," Ignatius laughed. He gave her more biscuits and a can of soda.

"Naturally," Mumbi said. "I bet this is a man's world," she added with a tinge of bitterness in her voice.

A man's world. It was the chief's favorite phrase. The words brought memories of her unpleasant encounter with him two weeks ago, flooding back to her mind. *Naturally, our friendship will remain our little secret. Here in the village, we don't have to do anything. We can always go to town—Karatina or Nyeri—when we need to have some fun. Nobody will ever find out. I guarantee you. And don't you worry about my age. Age is nothing but a number. In any case, if you are waiting for some young man in this village to be your friend, you might as well become a nun before it's too late, my dear. All the young men here are drug addicts. I can tell you that for free. In any case, what use is a broke young man? A girl needs a man with something in his pockets to take care of her needs. You know: all the beautiful little things a girl should be given by a man who loves her . . .*

Mumbi was suddenly strangely quiet as Ignatius showed them around the bunker. She was still thinking about the chief. *What did the old geezer take me for? A slut?* she wondered.

As they followed Ignatius around the winding burrow, she and Karoki couldn't help but marvel at the ingenuity that had gone into the making of the underground office complex. Small squares that looked like office cubicles opened into the corridor.

"This is the nerve centre of Black Devil's empire," Ignatius said, pushing open a door that led into a room with wall-to-roof shelves full of files. He picked up a file. Its cover said, "Confidential.".

"Here is a dossier on the Police Chief. It tells all about his dealings with Black Devil. All these files have similar information on almost every key personality in this country," Ignatius said with an expansive gesture. "Ngethe is the link man with most of the people. He also keeps the records."

"This one is on Chief Mageca," Karoki exclaimed, reading another slimmer file.

"Well," Ignatius said, "This is how the underworld coexists with the other world. The relationship here is symbiotic. It's like the relationship between a baby in the womb and its mother. Sometimes, I wonder where the dividing line is, if it exists at all."

"No wonder some criminals are untouchable," Karoki murmured.

Black Devil's earlier threats echoed chillingly through Karoki's mind: *I'll slice you up so fine that by the time I'm through with you, there won't be anything even for the maggots to feed on...* Now, having seen the various shades of his deviousness, Black Devil's threats did not ring as hollow as before. This was a man who was capable of every kind of evil. Certainly, Japheth knew what he was about when he nicknamed him *Black Devil.*

"You can imagine what would happen if all this came to light," Mumbi said. "A lot of fat cats would tumble down as if they had feet of straw."

"Yeah, there would be an earthquake in very high places," Karoki said. "Or maybe not," he grimly added.

"Maybe not? Why?" Mumbi said.

"Well!" he said and did not say anything more.

"Whatever that means," Mumbi said with a chuckle. "But seriously, I think this is a matter for the authorities to handle, don't you think?"

"I don't think they'll do much," Karoki said. "They might arrest him, but after a while, he'll be back in circulation."

"Frankly, I don't think anybody dares arrest that devil," Ignatius said.

"Come on, guys! So, what are you suggesting?" Mumbi was indignant. "We leave everything as it is?"

"Hell, no!" Karoki said.

"Thank you!" Mumbi cried. "We shouldn't be despondent. Despite everything, I believe there are still good people in the government who mean what they are saying. Besides, there are a lot of ordinary people who, just like us, would like to see these kinds of criminal activities eradicated from society. If push comes to shove, I believe they'll make their voices heard. After all, almost everybody is plenty fed up with this kind of lawlessness."

"Very well, but the question is: how do we move matters from push into shove, if you get what I mean?" Karoki asked.

"If we start thinking that way, we'll despair," Mumbi said. Then with a smile, she added, "You know what they say?"

"What?"

"They say that when it's time for the monkey to die, all the trees in the forest become slippery. Right now, all the trees in the forest are slippery for Black Devil and his fellow barons. You'll see. Everything will work itself out."

"And this new government you keep on talking about, what is it really about?" Ignatius asked.

"They are talking about zero tolerance of corruption," Mumbi said. "We'll see whether they mean it, or it's all just talk."

"Oh, what percentage did they tolerate before they started talking? Do you know?" Ignatius asked.

Karoki looked at him. A mischievous smile was playing on his lips. The man was not as dense as he had pretended to be when they first met him. *His grin is nothing but a mask,* Karoki thought.

"I don't know that," he said. "All I know is that they have declared a war on corruption. Maybe it's the same war your old friend back in Mwisho was waiting for?"

"That would be sad," Ignatius said with a chuckle. "The old geezer is long dead."

"Sad, nothing. The old man fought his wars. The current war is for us to fight, just as he fought his," Mumbi said. "Let's go, guys."

"I think we need to carry some of these files," Karoki suggested. "They are very juicy."

"Yeah, I think so, too," Mumbi agreed. A new idea occurred to her. "You know, I know a journalist—Amos Muriithi. He would give his life to get a hold of these files!"

"What would he do with the files if he's dead?" Karoki laughed. "But I see your point," he added soothingly. "If just a tad bit of the information in the files were published, the sun would drop out of the sky."

As they packed all the files in an empty sack, Mumbi thought of home. It was now almost twenty-four hours since she had left. Her parents must be beside themselves with worry, she thought.

"People in the village must be very worried," she said.

"Sure," Karoki agreed. "I think we need to get back home to save the old folks a lot of anxiety. The Grand Matriarch would die if she thought I was in trouble!"

"The Grand Matriarch? Is that some kind of a Goddess or what?"

"No. My grandmother," Karoki said. "But she amounts to the same thing, so I guess you're right."

"Oh, the grand old woman!" Mumbi exclaimed. "She's a very interesting lady. Every time she hears that somebody has died, she gets very depressed. She can't understand why children should die while she lives. 'How did I wrong God that I should live to see the children of my children dying?' she asks."

"You think she has a death wish?"

"No-oo!" Mumbi cried. "Only that some of the so-called children are almost in their eighties. She's a very sensitive woman. Very empathic."

"That's why I love her."

"That's why everyone loves her."

***

At the same time Karoki, Mumbi, and Ignatius were ransacking Black Devil's bunker, Mumbi's father was knocking on Chief Mageca's door. The elders had tasked him and Mwenda's mother to make a formal report about the missing youths and to seek assistance. His eyes darting restlessly behind the folds of fat on his flabby face, the chief met his visitors at the door. He was a big man—both physically and metaphorically—but this morning, his visitors did not show him the usual diffidence. And because the guilty are ever so suspicious, the chief thought his visitors' brashness had to do with Mumbi.

Just two weeks ago, he had made advances on Mumbi. It was a mistake. Her reaction had surprised and shocked him. Her stinging words were still ringing in his ears: *I don't mean to be insulting, but surely, bwana chief, you should be ashamed of yourself. You're even older than my father! You ought to behave with some dignity, and I hope you shall never force me to remind you that again.*

Now, as Chief Mageca greeted Ng'ang'a, he was full of apprehension. Could the girl have informed her father about his waywardness?

"Welcome Mr. Ng'ang'a," he said, trying to sound lively. "How are you, Mama Mwenda?" He glanced at his watch without really checking the time. "It's still quite early," he said. "I hope you come in peace."

"What peace, chief?" Mama Mwenda scoffed. "What peace, Chief, when our children disappear, and you can't be found to lend help?"

"It's alright, Mama Mwenda," Ng'ang'a said. "Our chief is a busy man."

"Yes, of course. I'm very busy. I have to attend a meetings at the County Headquarters."

"I understand," Ng'ang'a said. "But it's just as she has said. The children disappeared from the village, yesterday . . ."

"Yes, yesterday morning, Chief, and still no help from you!" Mama Mwenda cried.

"But really, how many times have I warned people against going into the forest?" the chief retorted, with a disdainful glance at the woman. "If parents will not take responsibility and help reign in their children, what can I do, even though I'm the chief?"

Ng'ang'a thought the chief was obfuscating. He said, "But you're a father, too, chief. You have children and grandchildren, and you know all about children. They hear with one ear, but often whatever you tell them goes right out through the other ear. Sometimes they bring you grief, but it's not that you haven't warned them. I think it's just how children are."

Chief Mageca only half-heard what Ng'ang'a was saying. He was still thinking about Mumbi. Not only had she rejected him, but she had also tried to humiliate him, the slut. *Now let's see if she can reject Pablo. Or try to humiliate him*, he thought.

"Well, maybe children are like that, but your daughter is not a child. Surely, you can't tell me she doesn't understand when we talk about the perils of the forest? Are you even sure that the youngsters are in the forest? I mean: is it not queer that a young woman and two young men can disappear, all at once? No, Mr. Ng'ang'a, something does not quite add up."

Ng'ang'a was indignant. Why was the chief trying to slur his daughter? Or did he know something that he was not letting on? Why the innuendoes?

"Our worst fear is that they might have been kidnapped," he said, still trying to keep calm. "You know, there are all sorts of stories, Chief. People talk about outlaws in the mountains."

There was a mean glint in Chief Mageca's eyes, but it flickered only for a moment before fizzling out. Ng'ang'a wasn't sure if he had imagined it.

"Who are these people that talk about such things, bwana Ng'ang'a? Isn't it a bit queer that they don't share what they know with me?"

The chief's patronising tone seemed to rattle Ng'ang'a. He suddenly jumped up to his feet. "Well, Chief," he said. "We are sending the search team back into the forest. We thought you might give us some policemen to assist in our search."

"That's all very well, Mr. Ng'ang'a. But the government works in certain ways. I'll make a report. In two to three days, it should reach the County Commissioner in Nyeri, who will decide if policemen should be sent to the forest. If he says yes, his word is my order. I'll go to the forest myself and find those youths."

"But Nyeri is just here—the distance between the eye and the nose!"

"The government has its way of doing things."

"But I thought all that had changed, now?" Ng'ang'a said.

"Oh, you thought so? Well, my friend. Government remains government. It doesn't matter who is in power."

"Alright, then. We'll look for our children. That's all we wanted to let you know—just in case," Ng'ang'a said. "Now, if you don't mind, we've got to go," he added and stormed out in a huff.

Gathering her skirts in her hand Mama Mwenda followed, hot on his heels. "Somebody has yet to tell me what kind of a chief we have in this village," she snorted, "Sometimes, I wonder if we would be better off without a chief!"

"Don't mind him," Ng'ang'a said. "Night runs until day catches up with him."

"Indeed."

Eight

When Karoki, Mumbi, and Ignatius all returned to the cave, they found Mwenda lying at the entrance with his knees drawn up to his chin. He was groaning softly, and his friends, realizing that something was very wrong, rushed to his side.

"What's the matter, man?" Mumbi asked, kneeling beside him.

"My stomach, it aches!" Mwenda cried.

"But why?"

Then, she saw the massive pile of fruit pulp all around him. She understood immediately. Mwenda had wolfed up so many fruits. *Could he have eaten some inedible, perhaps even poisonous fruit?* She wondered. Ignatius thought so too but, seemingly unfazed, he started picking up the pulp, scrutinizing each one carefully before dropping it. After a while, he whooped, holding up the pink pulp of an unknown fruit.

"This is the culprit," he said. "The fruit is as sweet as honey but bitter as bile to the stomach!"

Mumbi panicked when she remembered what Ignatius had said about the owl's hoot the previous night. "Is he in danger?" She gasped. "What shall we do now?"

"No, not in danger," Ignatius said. "We'll vomit him."

"Vomit him?" Mumbi echoed. "What do you mean?"

"He needs water, lots of it. Then we'll make him vomit. That'll dilute the poison in his blood. Wait, you'll see."

Ignatius picked up the boy, and placing him sideways across his shoulders, carried him to the riverside. Ignatius made him drink a lot of water. When he couldn't take in any more, Ignatius made him take some more.

"You could as well have drowned me in the river," Mwenda protested.

"No, I'm trying to make you drown the river," Ignatius chuckled, still giving him more of the water.

After he decided Mwenda had taken enough, Ignatius made him lie down on his side with his legs apart as if he were striding. Then, he went to work. Starting gently and then more and more vigorously, he pressed on Mwenda's stomach. Yellowish foul-smelling water gushed out through Mwenda's mouth and nostrils. Ignatius continued kneading Mwenda's stomach until nothing came out anymore.

"Now let him rest for a while," he said, finally, draping the boy with his old jungle jacket. "He'll be alright, don't worry," he added.

True to his word, Mwenda came around after a little while. But he still looked punctured and a little embarrassed. "I won't lie to you," he said sheepishly, looking around at his friends. "That was a close call—the second in as many days!"

"Then you had better watch out," Mumbi said.

But Karoki was unmoved. "I thought you're a tough nut," he taunted. "What happened to the spirit of the Rainbow Dragon, my friend? Was it to come to such an inglorious end, after all?"

"It's that accursed fruit," Mwenda sputtered. "Took the wind out of my sail and nearly sent me to my maker. But I still haven't yet lost grasp of the dragon's tail. So, the spirit lives on!"

He turned to Ignatius and said, "Thank you, buddy, for saving my life!"

"What's this spirit you guys always talk about?" Mumbi asked.

"The Spirit of the Rainbow Dragon!" Karoki replied.

"What is it all about?"

Mumbi listened with interest as Mwenda told her all about the rainbow dragon, and about the brave boy who had dared to pluck the magical hairs from the dragon's tail, shifting power onto a new, heroic generation.

"I'm heir to the spirit of the Rainbow Dragon through my grandfather," Mwenda said, proudly. "I never say die," he added.

But he realized that without his friends, and without Ignatius who had saved him from being poisoned, he may not have made it. And knowing that there was still so much they needed to do together before this whole saga was over, he added, "We are all three straighteners!"

"I see," Mumbi said. "You mean to say we are heirs to the spirit of the Rainbow Dragon?"

"Yes, yes," Mwenda readily agreed.

Karoki and Mumbi now told Mwenda all about the sprawling farms in the forest and Black Devil's bunker under the river. It was just as they had expected. Mwenda listened in awed silence. It was clear he regretted agreeing to be left behind.

"But did you find something that'll build our case against his gangs?" he asked, impatiently.

"Oh, yes, we did! More than you can ever imagine. Almost more than anybody could handle," Mumbi said.

Mwenda couldn't believe his eyes when they showed him the massive pile of files that they had brought back from the bunker.

"Black Devil is a sly manipulator," Karoki said. "He bribes key officials and then keeps meticulous records of the transactions. The aim is obviously to use the records for blackmail purposes. I think that's how he manages to keep all the officials beholden to him. They dare not make a move against him, lest he expose them," Karoki explained.

"That's spot-on," Ignatius said. "Black Devil swears that if the worst ever came to the worst, he'll never accept going down alone. It's no idle threat, either. He's just that kind of a man. He'll take down the world with him if it comes to that."

Ignatius's words were followed by an uneasy silence. It was as if his young friends were reflecting on how sad it would be if the world were to come to an end before they had lived long enough. But Ignatius was just as unperturbed as the river, which continued down its course as it had throughout the ages.

"Of course, that's nonsense," Karoki said. "I think Black Devil is just a megalomaniac."

"Well, I don't know that is," Ignatius grinned. "What I *do* know is that the man is capable of anything. He has no qualms; no qualms at all. In fact, I don't think it will be much use even giving him up to the police . . ."

"What? What are you talking about?" Mumbi exclaimed, suspiciously.

"If you ask me," Ignatius said, conspiratorially, "The best thing to do is to shoot and be done with him for good. Some people are better dead than alive."

"That would make us criminal, too," Karoki admonished.

"Then I've got a better idea still," Ignatius said. "How about I stop treating him and just let him die of his wounds?"

"Listen, Ignatius," Karoki gruffly said, "The last thing we want is for Black Devil to die. Dead men tell no tales. You've got to understand that he's more useful alive than dead. Otherwise, we would have shot all of you a long time ago!"

"I agree," Mumbi said. "If he's dead, that means his associates might never be exposed."

Ignatius shrugged his shoulders nonchalantly. "I see your point," he said. "My fear is if the other barons find out that he's here. They'll come for him; make no mistake about that. Then, all of us will join the buffalo in the vultures' guts!"

All of them grew quiet. Nobody had thought about such a possibility. Now that Ignatius had brought it up, it seemed not only likely but looming. Suddenly, Mwenda, Karoki, and Mumbi all felt like sitting ducks. Danger seemed to lurk in every shadow—behind every bush. Even the drone of the river seemed to carry with it an ominous and strident message: *GET OUT OF HERE BEFORE IT'S TOO LATE!*

The nearest police station was in Karatina, a small bustling town some fifty kilometers away. Karoki revealed that he had money on him—enough for their fare to Karatina, once they got to the road. Ignatius swung the heavy sack of files onto his shoulders.

"We don't have to go through the village," he said. "I know a shortcut through the forest to the main road. It's much faster."

"Remember—no tricks," Karoki warned.

"Aw, man," Ignatius protested. "You're such a bore. I thought that was all behind us, now?"

"Not until this whole thing is behind us," Karoki said.

***

The search team from the village entered the forest on one side, just as Ignatius, Mwenda, Karoki, Mumbi, and their prisoners exited the forest on the other side. Enraged by the noncommittal response from the chief and armed with whatever weapons they could lay their hands on, scores of people had joined the search team. The young men of Hombe village had finally decided to take matters into their own hands.

Sensing trouble and fearing the worst, the elders could no longer sit on their laurels. They decided to send a delegation of people to Karatina town to see the sub-county commissioner and the local police commander. If the chief would not help, maybe his seniors could.

Meanwhile, dressed in Ignatius's jungle jacket, Mwenda looked like a hardened teenage soldier from some backwater war zone. When he and his team reached the road, they made their prisoners sit in the grass by the roadside. Mwenda concealed his gun underneath his heavy jacket. In a short while, a *matatu* appeared, speeding down the road. Mumbi flagged it down. It skidded to a stop, and a tout jumped out. "Karatina! Karatina town!" he shouted.

"Come on, get in!" Mwenda ordered the prisoners. The tout looked at the men with curious interest as they stood up.

"What have they done?" he asked.

"We found them growing illegal drugs in the forest," Mumbi said.

The tout seemed taken aback. "You mean they are the infamous gangs?"

"Yes, part of the gangs."

"Oh, what a shame," the tout said. There was not the slightest hint of outrage in his voice. In fact, he looked as if he would not mind a few rolls of bhang if somebody gave them to him. He was unkempt, and his eyes were like strawberries: so bloodshot.

"So, you're taking them to where?"

"To the police station," Mumbi said.

The tout looked at Black Devil, who was glaring at him, and said, "Till we meet again, pal."

"What do you mean, till we meet again?" Black Devil erupted. "Do you know me?"

"It doesn't matter," the tout said. "You're going in for a very long, long time. This government is no joke. You ought to have known better."

He turned to Karoki, who was sitting in the seat just behind the driver. "Three hundred bob."

"What's that?"

"The fare," the tout said, rather gruffly.

"Oh, I see!" But when he looked for his money, Karoki could not find it. It seemed like he had lost it. "I swear I had a five hundred note in my pocket," he said.

"Hey, Joe. What story is that you've started?"

"It's true. I had the money."

"I don't care what you had," the tout said, really hostile now. "Give me my money or get out!"

"We've got dangerous criminals here. Please help us get them to the police station," Mumbi pleaded.

"Yeah," Karoki chipped in. "It's just a small sacrifice."

Most of the passengers agreed that it was just a small sacrifice. They were impressed when they heard how the teenagers had managed to arrest the thugs on their own. But the crew was still adamant. They were in business—and not inclined to make sacrifices. Suddenly, the driver applied the brakes. The vehicle shuddered and stopped right in the middle of the road. A lorry following closely behind swerved to avoid bumping into the *matatu*. As it overtook the *matatu*, the loader leaned out of the cabin and hurled unspeakable epithets at the *matatu* driver.

"Let them get out," the *matatu* driver said.

"No, we won't," Karoki said.

"You won't?"

"Make us if you can."

"I will!"

The tout started to pull out Mumbi, who was nearest the door. The passengers protested, timidly. The driver jumped out of his seat, flourishing a whip. At the sight of the flog, Mumbi visibly shrunk. Karoki scrambled out of the vehicle and whipped out his pistol. At the sight of the gun, the tout fled. He leapt over the fence and into the weltering farmlands by the roadside, disappearing into the wilting maize crop.

"Get back into the vehicle!" Karoki ordered the driver.

The man did as ordered.

"You know the Karatina police station, of course?"

"Yes."

"Now drive there—directly!"

And so, the vehicle rattled down the road. At the junction to Karatina town, two traffic policemen stood on the shoulder of the road. One was reading a newspaper. For once, the driver hoped they would stop him. They did.

"Mind now!" Karoki whispered as the policeman came up, "If you mention anything or try to be clever in any way, I'll blow out your brains faster than you can say *gun*. Try me."

The driver shot him an angry look. He folded a fifty-shilling note and slipped it into his driver's license. Then, the policeman shook hands with the driver, and the man gave him his license. The policeman went to the front of the vehicle, pretending he was checking the insurance sticker on the windshield. Then he came back and handed the driver his license and waved him on without a word.

Karoki caught a glimpse of the headline in the newspaper the policeman was holding. It read: "SENIOR ADMINISTRATORS, POLICE CHIEFS REPLACED IN MAJOR RESHUFFLE." Karoki guessed that the headline had to do with the ongoing war against corruption. But still thinking about the dirty little game he had just witnessed, a wave of something akin to despair came over Karoki. The war against corruption was not going to be won easily.

The driver was the first one to jump out of the vehicle at the police station. He angrily stormed the report office, shouting that he had been carjacked. The two young constables sprang to their feet as if they had springs in their legs.

" Carjacked?"

"Yes, by two armed young rascals and a girl!" The driver yelled. "Come on, they are in my *matatu*!"

The two policemen grabbed their guns and rushed to the door. After peeping through the crack between the frame and the door, one of them rushed towards the *matatu*, gun drawn.

"Stay in your seats until ordered otherwise," he thundered.

Mumbi, who had been struggling to open the rusty door, went stiff. A chill rippled down her spine. The policeman forced the door open and ordered the passengers to alight, one by one. Mumbi was the first to get out. The policeman swiftly trained his gun on her. She could guess what the driver must have told the policemen.

"What's the matter, officer?" She tried to smile.

"She's the girl; she's one of the hijackers!" The driver shouted.

"No, sir," Mumbi protested. "We brought you criminals. Real ones. The driver is just unhappy. He would not cooperate, so we made him."

The policeman did not want to, but he almost believed her. The girl looked too—he couldn't find the right words—naïve? Innocent?

"Brought criminals? Where are they?" The second policeman asked.

"Here!" Mwenda shouted from the back of the vehicle, where he was waiting for his charges to get out ahead of him. "But you can relax, officer. Everything is under control."

As the captives clumsily scrambled out of the vehicle, the officer noticed that their hands were trussed. They were dirty and looked rough in a rugged sort of way. *They must be the criminals*, he thought. Coming out behind the men, Mwenda looked so comical in his big, jungle jacket that the policemen could not help but laugh.

Mwenda removed his jacket. He handed over his gun and the machete he had kept strapped to his belt to the policeman. Karoki too handed over his gun.

"This is . . . this is interesting!" The first policeman said, marvelling at the weapons. "Now, son, could you tell us how you got hold of these weapons?"

"It's a long story, sir," Mwenda said, knowing that his explanation must sound as unbelievable as Ignatius's and Ngethe's stories back in the forest.

A sergeant emerged from the office. He was unnecessarily aggressive. "What stories are you talking about?" He demanded. "This is not a place for stories!"

"Sir, let me explain," Mwenda pleaded.

"Don't worry. You'll have plenty of time for that," the sergeant said. "You guys have got a lot of explaining to do, anyway," he added.

The sergeant ordered the officers to search the vehicle. Then, he briefly questioned the rest of the passengers before allowing them to go on with their journey.

As the *matatu* left the police station, the driver leaned out of the window and gestured insultingly. "I hope they lock the three of you up and throw away the keys!" he said.

"It's alright," Mwenda called back, chuckling. "We live on hope!"

Nine

The delegation of elders had hardly left for Karatina when one of Chief Mageca's informers rushed into his home. Gakunia was widely known in the village as the chief's ear to the ground. He was a middle-aged man of about fifty five and one of those people—you know them, of course—who derive a peculiar pleasure from causing trouble for others. He thrived on spying on his fellow villagers, collecting tidbits here and there, which he would embellish and later offer to any officer who cared to listen. Sometimes, he managed to cause a lot of trouble for some villagers and was, for this reason, the most unpopular man in the village.

Chief Mageca was having breakfast when he heard his front gate click open. He went to the window, which faced towards the gate, and spied Gakunia entering his compound. Returning to the table, he took one boiled egg that remained on his plate to the kitchen.

"Keep this for me," he said to his wife, "I'll eat it later. Gakunia comes!"

"I thought he was your friend," Mrs. Mageca laughed, with a dry, caustic chuckle that dripped with disdain. It was hard to decide who she resented the most—her own husband or Gakunia.

"He is a loafer and a pauper!" Chief Mageca retorted. "He doesn't have a single hen in his whole compound. All he does is loiter and spread rumors like a virus all over. I wonder: what brings him now?"

"How should I know what you talk about with him?"

"He's a tiresome gossiper."

"Don't they say it takes two to tango?"

Chief Mageca returned to the table when Gakunia knocked on the door.

"*Karibu*," his wife said, welcoming the visitor. "Come right in."

"How are you, Son of Ihuru?" Gakunia said, genially shaking hands with the chief.

"I'm not complaining," the chief replied. "What's the news in the village?"

"News? I see you forget our ways," Gakunia grumbled. "Since when did you ask a hungry man for news?"

"Oh, yes," the chief said. "First things first."

He asked for a cup and poured his friend some tea. "It's not that anybody is hungry," Gakunia said. "It's what the white man calls *etiquette*. Of course, you don't expect even a cup of tea if you go to his house unannounced, but our customs are different. We may not have much, but we share. We know a guest is like a river, just passing by. Let people not forget our cherished ways."

"True. True indeed," the chief agreed. "So, what is the news?"

"Have you heard about what the elders have done?" Gakunia said, lowering his voice, conspiratorially.

"It's about those kids, isn't it? Well, I know the elders wanted to send a search team into the forest. I told them to wait until the County Commissioner gives directions on the matter," Mageca said.

"Really? They have sent a battalion into the forest!"

"A battalion? What do you mean?"

"Well, what else do you call it when every young man takes up arms and storms the forest, agemate?"

Chief Mageca felt his heart leap, then start racing. A cold sweat broke out on his brow. He wiped it with a crumpled old handkerchief. Gakunia eyed him closely and sipped his tea.

"Are you not going to give me something to eat along with this tea?" he asked, longingly eyeing the eggshells and arrow-root peels that Mageca's wife had forgotten or maybe neglected to remove from the table. "It's too hot. Scalds the mouth."

The extortioner! Mageca thought indignantly. Still, knowing that Gakunia would withhold crucial information if not appeased, he called his wife over and asked her to give his friend something to eat with the tea. She gave him the egg that her husband had returned into the kitchen just a moment ago.

"So, you say that the youths have already gone into the forest?"

"Yes, I came as soon as they left."

"How could they make such a reckless move?"

"My friend, many times I've told you to watch that man called Ng'ang'a closely. I tell you: that man does not wish you a long and healthy life," Gakunia said. "Have you heard that he might actually replace you as chief?"

"What are you saying?" Chief Mageca asked, scandalized. "Are people sick? Who's spreading such rumors?"

As a matter of fact, there were no rumors in the village about Ng'ang'a taking over as chief. Gakunia had picked them up at the County Headquarters in Nyeri.

"Rumors? If you're not careful, my friend, that man will eat your arrowroots for Christmas!" Gakunia pointedly said. "I don't know what wrong you've done to him," he added with a mischievous wink which meant he knew about Chief's Mageca's former interest in Ng'ang'a's daughter.

Chief Mageca would not be drawn into talking about that. He was still thinking about his job. Lately, his new boss at the sub-county headquarters didn't seem quite as friendly towards him, and with some senior administrators already shuffled aside, it was just a matter of time before the bloom swept low. He thought about Ng'ang'a. Although it was true that a chief must come from the village, Ng'ang'a a was just a simple villager from a very poor family. He had some education—true—but as far as Mageca knew, not the kind of connections that would smooth his way to the office. And without those, there was really nothing he could do. That's just not how the world worked.

"That poor man is a dreamer," he said.

"That may well be so, my friend," Gakunia replied, evenly, "But when I see him inciting the elders to go and complain to the District Officer, what am I supposed to think? Am I not your friend?"

"Complain to the D.O.?" Mageca demanded.

"Have I suddenly stammered, my friend? How is it I don't seem to be understood?"

"But that's going too far!"

"Exactly," Gakunia said. "And who knows how far or high he might go? What's to stop him from going all the way to the County Commissioner?"

"That peasant?"

"Yes. And why not? This government is encouraging people to speak out. It seems that nowadays, anybody can walk into any office to complain. Look at what happened in Murang'a the other day. . ."

But Mageca was already gone. He stormed into his bedroom. When he emerged moments later, he was stuffed into his full uniform, which was getting too small for him, thanks to his extra weight.

"What do you intend to do?"

"I am going to Karatina. I must see Mr. D.O. The villagers surely can't see him without my authority!" Mageca raved. He went to the kitchen and told his wife that he was leaving. Accompanied by Gakunia, he left, but when he reached the gate, he remembered something and went back into the house.

In the kitchen, he took a jar full of flour from the cupboard and measured out three cups. "This will be enough for lunch?" he asked his wife. The woman shrugged her shoulders indifferently. Mageca measured out one more cup. "There will only be you and the farmhand at home for lunch," he said, levelling the remainder of the flour into the jar. "People shouldn't eat like ants!"

His wife did not speak.

Mageca pressed his big hand on the flour, printing it on the flour in the jar. When he returned from Karatina, he would check the jar. If the print was not there, he would know that his wife had taken more flour. Then . . .

"Let's go, my friend," he said, rejoining Gakunia at the gate. "I had forgotten to give my wife something for lunch."

The two men walked fast and in silence. By the time they reached the small shopping centre, Mageca was snorting and sweating profusely. They were lucky. There was an almost full *matatu* ready to leave for town.

***

Chief Inspector Omar Hassan was the police commandant. He had left the office earlier for some errands in the town. After that, he had passed by the mosque for his midday prayers, as he was a devout Muslim. Now, as he drove back to the office, he felt satiated both in body and spirit. For the three months he had been at Karatina, Inspector Omar had been laying the groundwork for a major security operation.

When he took over as Commandant, Inspector Omar found a lot of intelligence reports in the office about the drug barons of Mount Kenya. Inspector Omar was surprised that no action had ever been taken against them, although they were all well-known. When he asked his intelligence officer about this, however, the man suddenly looked very nervous.

"*Afande*," he said, clearly worried. "Nobody moves against the drug moguls. The last time somebody tried, he nearly lost his job."

"Lost his job?"

"Almost. In the end, they transferred him all the way to North Eastern!"

"Where in North Eastern?"

"Mandera," the man said. "I'm told it's a very difficult place to work—actually, a hardship area."

The way the man spoke, it was like North Eastern was another name for hell.

"Well, I come from North Eastern myself, so being transferred there would actually be like sending a camel to the desert," Inspector Omar said. "And don't forget. Even those who live there are also Kenyans. They have a right to government services, too," he added curtly.

"I'm sorry, sir," the officer said apologetically. "I didn't mean it that way. What I really meant to say is that those drug people seem to have cronies in very high places."

"Are they higher than Allah?"

"God forbid that I should say that!"

Inspector Omar smiled.

But it was true what the intelligence man said. The issue of those farms in the forest was taboo. Nobody wanted to touch it. Inspector Omar had only recently found one ally in the newly-appointed District Officer. A fresh graduate from the University, the new D.O. was young and, like all young men, idealistic and perhaps a little naïve. But he still had an enthusiasm for his job that Inspector Omar sorely respected.

As far as Inspector Omar was concerned, it was simply immoral to defile the forest. The mountain which the forest covered was the crown of Kenya, a bedecked crown. At the foot of the mountain, thousands of visitors from all over the world bowed their reverence every year, just like the local people had done for centuries. It surely deserved to be treated with some respect. Then, there was the question of drugs. Anyone who dealt in drugs was the worst of criminals. After all, look at all devastation they brought, especially to the youth.

As he approached the police station, Inspector Omar felt a little lilt of excitement. His plan was almost complete. "God willing, I shall stop the growing of bhang in the forest," he promised himself.

At the gate, cries jolted the inspector's mind.

You should let me explain. Let me explain!

Somebody was crying. The voice sounded like that of a boy.

"What is the trouble now?" Inspector Omar asked himself, aloud. He swerved his Land Rover into the compound and brought it to a halt in front of the office.

A strange boy was on the ground, jostling with an officer. Constable Kabanya was holding the obstinate boy by the belt, trying to yank him to his feet. Corporal Mutua and three other officers stood aside, enjoying the show. The unexpected arrival of the boss threw them into confusion.

"What's going on?" Inspector Omar demanded.

"They won't let me explain!" Mwenda said, jumping to his feet.

"It's some kids, Sir," Corporal Mutua said, "They were brought in, accused of trying to hijack a *matatu*. They were armed, sir, with two guns and a machete. They claim to have arrested some marijuana growers in the forest . . ."

"It's not a claim, sir. It is a fact," Mwenda interjected. "And we did not hijack the *matatu*. We just asked the driver to help us bring the men here. He was not very enthusiastic, so we had to persuade him. So, that's why he said we hijacked his *matatu*," Mwenda grinned.

"Persuade him?" Inspector Omar smiled. "How did you do that if I may ask?"

"They were armed, sir," the corporal said.

"Sir, we took the pistol from Black Devil's security man," Mwenda said. "The old gun we found in the Mau Mau caves is practically useless. The only other thing we had was a machete, the same one that farmers use in the fields. We have handed over everything to the police."

Black Devil!

The familiar name hit the Inspector like a sledgehammer—stunned him. The name was in every 'Top Secret' intelligence report he had ever read. Black Devil, whoever he was, was one of the most notorious bhang growers up the mountain. A leading drug lord in the country. The reports he had read associated Black Devil with many other crimes—some dating years back, when he was just starting his life of debauchery.

Inspector Omar recalled one particular case in which Black Devil was suspected of killing a certain driver in a car smuggling deal. He had been questioned by the police, but they apparently couldn't directly link him to the murder. The trail had led to a man by the name of Ignatius, who was suspected of having been Black Devil's hireling. But it was like the man had evaporated from the face of the earth. The police speculated that he too may have been eliminated in Kisumu, his body probably fed to the crocodiles of Lake Victoria.

"Did you say Black Devil, boy?" Inspector Omar asked.

"Yes, sir," Mwenda replied. "We arrested him in the mountains."

"You did what?!"

"We arrested him, sir."

"Yes, sir," the corporal said. "The alleged Black Devil is in the cell."

Inspector Omar went to the cells. He ordered that Karoki be freed immediately. Then, the three youths went with the inspector to the cells. When he saw the suspects, he did not have to think twice. There was nothing *alleged* about the big, dark man who stared back at him through his one good eye. Everything about him fitted the same profile that was in the intelligence reports.

"You're Black Devil, of course?"

"No. My name is Pablo. And I need to talk to my doctor and my lawyers."

"We'll see about that—in the fullness of time," Inspector Omar said off-handedly and mused, "Pablo? That's an interesting name."

"And this, sir, is our friend, Ignatius," Mwenda said, introducing the man who he'd come to like.

"Oh!" The Inspector cried. "Ignatius, might you be the guy who . . .in Kisumu?"

"Yes, sir. The very same one."

"Are you sure you're not his ghost?"

"Ghost, sir? No. I'm Ignatius himself. But I did not kill Sammy. No, sir."

"I didn't say *you* killed anybody, did I?" Inspector Omar regarded the two men searchingly. "Now, this is getting very interesting indeed," he said, finally.

In his office, Inspector Omar questioned Mwenda, Karoki, and Mumbi closely, all the time flipping through the files that they had brought back from the forest. One main file drew his interest. He whistled in astonishment as he read.

"Corporal, please ask Sergeant Pesa to come over."

The corporal went out and returned a moment later with the Sergeant. Inspector Omar stood up as they came in. For the first time, Mwenda noticed how tall he was and how the Inspector dwarfed all the other officers.

"Sergeant Pesa . . ." Inspector Omar said.

"Sir!" The Sergeant smartly saluted.

"You're under arrest!"

"Sir?"

Even the other officers were taken aback by the unexpected turn of events.

"Yes, go ahead. Put him in," Inspector Omar said to the men.

"But what have I done, sir?" The sergeant cried as his colleagues pounced on him.

"Well, boss," Corporal Mutua said, leading the sergeant away. "To the cells!"

"But what have I done? I've got a right to know why I'm being arrested."

"Don't know," the corporal shrugged, "But as you always say, orders are given to be followed. I'm just following my orders."

"Idiot!"

Ten

When the elders finally arrived at Karatina, they learned that a new D.O. had recently been posted to the office. Mzee Gatama, the oldest of the men, was a little worried. The new D.O. was not of their tribe. Would he still listen to them?

"You know, the only person who empathizes with a child's pain is the parent," the old man said. "How could this new D.O. be expected to be moved by the plight of three lost children who were neither of his ridge nor clan?"

The old men deliberated on this issue for a while. The driver of their hired pickup truck, a young man of about thirty, listened from a respectful distance. When he found a chance to put in a word, he said, "My fathers, I don't think you should worry about whether the D.O. will help or not. I believe he will help. That's his job."

"Gatimu is right," Ng'ang'a said, coming to the aid of the driver, "Of course, one must always belong to his clan and tribe, but government officers are not supposed to carry their tribes into office. Not anymore, otherwise, why did we vote for a new government? Was it not because we wanted to be treated as one people? We cannot judge the officer before we meet him. He, too, is a Kenyan, same as us."

"That's what I was trying to say," Gatimu said.

In the office, a beautiful young secretary with a pleasant smile received the elders. Ng'ang'a presented their case. He told of their fear that the three lost youths might have strayed into the bhang farms in the forest, where they could be kidnapped by the drug barons.

"And your chief is aware?" The secretary asked.

"Yes, we saw him about the matter," Ng'ang'a said.

He explained about their visit to the chief and what the chief had said. The young lady listened patiently, occasionally jotting some notes into a small book. When Ng'ang'a finished, the lady excused herself and disappeared into an inner office. A few moments later, she reappeared and ushered the men into the office she had just left.

District Officer Aggrey Simatei met the elders at the door. He was a young man in his thirties. He was very friendly.

"My secretary has informed me about your case," he said, straightaway. "I've heard about those bhang farms in the mountains, and it has been my intention to uproot them and, if possible, arrest the growers. In fact, I've just been consulting with the local police commandant over the issue. Chief Inspector Omar and I have been planning an operation to rid the forest of the growers, once and for all. But now, it seems we must move fast. We must find these children."

"That's all we ask," Mzee Muhoro said in his faltering Kiswahili, "That the government should help us find our children."

The phone rang, and the D.O. picked it up. Inspector Omar Hassan was on the line. "How are you, Inspector?"

"Stop the niceties, and come over here as soon as you can," Inspector Omar said, "It's an emergency!"

"I've got a rather serious case over here too," D.O. Simatei said, "Some youngsters have gotten lost in the forest, and I've got a delegation of elders from Hombe village who want us to help them find the youths."

"That's why I'm calling you," Inspector Omar said, "The young fellows are in my office right now. We've been upstaged. They've arrested Black Devil and unearthed quite a lot of useful information."

"Heck, what do you mean they've arrested Black Devil? How?"

"It's a long story," Inspector Omar said. "Sounds like stuff from the movies. You've got to hear the whole story from them," Inspector Omar said. "But the thing is: it seems that the criminals have infiltrated our whole security system. I've already had to detain one of my senior officers."

And as the D.O. and the inspector spoke, Chief Mageca entered the office, breathless and snorting like a pig. Speaking sideways, the D.O. welcomed his chief in before continuing, "That's alright, Inspector. Chief Mageca has just come in. I think he'll help us . . ."

"That's the Hombe chief?"

"Yes, Inspector. He's one of our senior and most experienced chiefs—"

"Detain him immediately."

"Inspector?"

"From what I can see, he needs to tell us a bit more about the going-ons in the forest," Inspector Omar said. "It seems your predecessor and the chief were quite intimate with the forest gangs. Just put him in, and please do come over. We need to move fast. I'm told there are some useful documents in the forest. We need to retrieve them before somebody upstages us again. And of course, I think this is the right time to destroy the marijuana farms. But come, I'll tell you more when we meet."

"Alright."

The D.O. put down the phone with a sigh. He pressed a bell on his desk, and his secretary came in. "Please get me Sergeant Opoyo," he said.

Presently, Sergeant Opoyo, an administration police officer attached to the D.O.s office, came in. He saluted and greeted the old men.

"Sergeant, please show Chief Mageca a place to rest," the D.O. said.

Chief Mageca almost fell down to the floor. The last time the D.O. said that, somebody was put in the cells. Even Sergeant Opoyo seemed confused, but of course, orders were orders.

"Bwana D.O.," Chief Mageca said. "Why would you want to arrest me?"

"Let's talk about that later," the D.O. said. "For now, we have to go and put an end to the dirty little things you and your friends have been doing in the forest."

Even though they didn't like him much, all the villagers were a little shaken to see their own chief arrested, right in front of their eyes. Truly, the government worked in strange ways.

Chief Mageca lost his cool as he was led away. "I have been framed, Mr. District Officer!" he protested. "Somebody wants my job, I know it!"

"Who wants your job?"

"He's sitting right in front of you—that man, Ng'ang'a!"

The D.O. was surprised. How had Chief Mageca gotten wind of his impending replacement? He tried not to show it, however. "Maybe it's about time we gave your job to somebody else, too," he said. He regarded the chief somberly and added: "We surely need a chief who will not get into league with the devil just to destroy government forests. You know what I mean?"

"I'm a chief, not a forest officer!"

"Well, you *were* a chief."

"That boy, Kiongo: it seems like he has more sense than all of us, after all," Mzee Muhoro said reflectively.

"It seems so," Ng'ang'a said. "He always said *kikulacho ki nguoni mwako*. It's a shame we never took him seriously."

"Yes, a real shame," Mzee Muhoro agreed.

*****

Following the D. O.'s convoy of vehicles full of policemen, the elders in their rusty hired pickup drove to the police station. Meanwhile, Inspector Omar was pacing up and down in front of his office. Three jeeps with more policemen were parked nearby. Inspector Omar had been waiting for the D. O.'s team. As soon as they arrived, he held brief consultations with the D.O., and then, the whole squad was ready to move to the forest.

The elders could not go into the forest, of course, but Mumbi, Karoki, and Mwenda were adamant. They still wanted to join the police in the operation. After some arguing, Inspector Omar agreed that they could. They had inspired the operation, and they would be allowed to see it to its conclusion.

"There is one condition though," Inspector Omar said. "You must keep in the background and well out of the way."

Over the moon with excitement, Mumbi, Karoki, and Mwenda only half-heard what the inspector was saying. "It's really about your safety," he insisted. "Things can get really ugly in an operation, very ugly!"

"Yes, yes!" they cried out in unison, "Whatever you say!"

"Mind you," Inspector Omar smiled, "I can arrest you if you endanger your life!"

"Aw, how come, now?" Mwenda laughed. "It's my life, after all."

"Is that what you think?" Inspector Omar smiled. "Well, I've news for you, my boy. Your life belongs to the government of Kenya. You're not allowed to endanger it needlessly. And there'll be consequences if you do. Mark my words!"

Mwenda shrugged.

Later, the convoy stopped at a petrol station. Inspector Omar gave the three youths a two hundred shillings note.

"I know you may not have eaten for a while," he said, "Buy yourself something to eat."

Mumbi, Karoki, and Mwenda were grateful, but fearing that the inspector wanted to shake them off, they agreed that Mumbi would go buy something while the boys kept an eye on the convoy.

Although there was a café just across the road, Mumbi ran almost halfway across the town, cutting through the big open-air market to The Mountain Stripes Hotel. This hotel was popular with politicians and other movers and shakers in the town. It was here that Amos and the other journalists whiled away the time when they were not out of town on assignments. Mumbi prayed that she might be lucky enough to find him.

She had just walked into the hotel when somebody called her name. Mumbi saw Amos waving at her from a seat near the window overlooking the street, in the same place they had sat once upon a time. He was sitting with some men and looked surprised to see her. As always, whenever she saw him, her heart lurched, and a strange excitement came over her. She walked over to where he was and said, "It's you I'm looking for, man!"

"What is it, Mumbi?" Amos asked, looking flustered. "Something wrong?"

"You are such a worrier," Mumbi said with a chuckle. "No, nothing wrong. But come on. I'll tell you what's up."

Amos picked his backpack from the floor.

"There goes a man in a lot of trouble!" One of the men said as Amos excused himself and followed the girl out of the hotel.

"What's this I'm hearing about some lads from your village, lost in the forest?" Amos asked when they came out into the street.

Mumbi laughed and said, "We've been found."

"You were among them?"

"Yes."

Amos was incredulous. He looked her over. It was only then that he noticed how shabby she was.

"Christ! What happened? You run into trouble with the outlaws?"

"Almost did. But we outwitted them," Mumbi said. "That's why I wanted to see you. We're going to the forest! Inspector Omar and the D.O. are going to destroy the bhang farms."

"Surely you're not pulling my leg?"

"But why should I? See those police jeeps over there? That's Inspector Omar. We're going to the forest right now. I thought you'd want to join us in action."

"Like hell, I would!"

They walked over to the petrol station.

"Aye!" Amos said to Inspector Omar in greeting.

"Aye," Inspector Omar said and laughed.

"I smell a big story, Inspector," Amos said.

"Yes, a very big one—an earth-shaking story!"

Suddenly Amos grasped Inspector Omar's hand. He seemed strangely excited, and his hand shook a little. "My friend," he said, "You'll let me into this, won't you?"

"What do you mean?"

"I mean, you won't give this story to the big boys in Nairobi. You'll give a local boy his big break?"

"I don't understand . . ."

"You know that every time we've got big stories, they always, somehow, end up being handled by the big journalists from Nairobi. How are we, poor stringers, ever going to break into the big leagues?"

"Oh, I see," Inspector Omar said. "But don't worry. If you're ready to cross the Rubicon, I've got very titillating stuff for you."

"I am equal to the task. Trust me," said Amos, smiling. "Every morning I ask God to give me strength equal to my challenges, not challenges equal to my strength!" He joked.

What a humorous man, Mumbi thought.

"That's wise of you," Inspector Omar beamed, "Otherwise, being the small man you are, you would be doomed to always handle small challenges!"

Everybody laughed.

So, Amos jumped into the jeep along with the others. Mumbi introduced Amos to her friends. "This is Karoki, and this is Mwenda, the bird. These are the lost and found guys," she said. "And this is my friend, Amos Muriithi. He's the journalist I was telling you about."

Amos shook hands with the boys. As they drove, the boys munched on their chips and sausages and regaled everybody with the story of their adventures in the forest. Amos listened with interest as they told him about how they were heirs to a strange spirit that they called the Spirit of the Rainbow Dragon.

"What spirit is that, kids?" one of the policemen asked, without much interest.

"The spirit of those who straighten up things!" Mwenda said.

"That's interesting," Amos said. "Maybe after this, you'll tell me a bit more about the spirit?"

"For your newspaper?"

"Yes, for my newspaper."

"You'll take our photos and put us in the paper?" Mwenda asked.

"Sure. In the *Quencher*."

"You hear, *wasee*," Mwenda said to his friends, excitedly. "We'll be in the paper!"

Eleven

Kiongo and his team were tired. After finding a heap of fruit pulp lying near one of the caves by the river and signs of fire in the cave nearby, it had seemed like finding the children would be a quick success. However, after searching the forest all morning, they were now on the verge of despair. So, they sat down to rest. Some of the men thought that the youngsters could have gone back to the village by another route. The more pessimistic feared the worst.

"Maybe they strayed into the marijuana farms, and the gangs made a clean job of them…"

"What do you mean—made a clean job of them?"

Kanyua made a slashing gesture across his neck with his machete and twisted his mouth in feigned agony.

"Ai, man," Kiongo admonished. "Don't talk like that!"

"What do we do then, boss?"

"I think we've got to go to the farms. We might discover something," Kiongo said. "I don't believe that the outlaws would go as far as killing three harmless teenagers. They wouldn't want to provoke the ire of the village. I don't think they would dare, anyway."

"And why wouldn't they? Criminals are criminals. Chief Mageca says these men are dangerous and quite reckless."

"Oh, forget the old goat!" Kiongo said, impatiently. "The man is a scaremonger. I've never believed one word he says about those so-called gangs."

"The man is only good at seducing other people's wives, that's all," Ngaita said.

"Yes, people's wives and daughters, intimidating them with the crown," Kiongo spat.

"You heard he has something going on with Mumbi?"

"What?" Kiongo exclaimed.

"I heard it from the horse's own mouth!"

"From Mumbi?"

"No."

"From Mageca?"

"No."

"Hell. So, what do you mean from the horse's own mouth?"

"I heard it from Gakunia. He knows everything about the chief. Doesn't he?" Ngaita said.

"Yes, he does. The two are like brothers. Born of the same ogre."

A noisy flight of weaver birds flew overhead. Following them with his eyes, Kiongo felt his mind take flight along with the birds. Was it really true that something was going between her and the chief? How was it possible when she had told him herself that she would not *think* of a man, any man before she realized her heart's desire to go to medical college? And even if she were so double-faced, would she stoop so low as to entertain a mannerless billy goat like Mageca?

Then the most frightening thought crossed Kiongo's mind. It seemed so self-evident now that he could not understand why he had not thought about it before. Mumbi had rejected the old goat—what else could any girl do?—and the chief had unleashed his thugs in the forest on her. Chief Mageca was just the kind of man who would relish that kind of vengefulness.

"What are the birds saying?" Kanyua said with a chuckle, nudging Kiongo out of his reverie.

Kiongo smiled as if he had secret knowledge. Without a word, he abruptly rose and said, "Let's go to the farms."

But only five men rose along with him.

"I think if we go, we'll need to get the police first," Kanyua said.

"But Chief Mageca will not give us policemen," Kiongo said. "You heard what he said?"

"Yes, but we can get policemen from Karatina."

"Yeah, we can, but the elders are already there," Kiongo said. "If the police want to come, then they are probably already on their way. Maybe they've even already arrived in the forest."

"I think—" Kanyua started.

"Oh!" Kiongo cut him short, "Seems like you'll be thinking till thy kingdom come!"

Another man said, "But I think Kanyua has a point. We can't face men with guns with machetes. Can we?"

"Yes, of course, we can," Kiongo gruffly said. "It will not be the first time in history that has happened. Besides, it's not about blindly facing the thugs. We've got to have a strategy and some wits."

"I think—"

"If we are all thinkers here, then maybe we should just go back home and tell everybody that we chickened out," Kiongo said, impatiently. "What we need right now are men—guys who are ready to *do* for a change."

"I guess you're right."

"So, if I'm right and you're man enough, come with me."

With that, Kiongo started to walk. Six men followed him. Before they disappeared into the forest, Kiongo turned to all the men who had remained behind and said, "When you get home, make sure Grandmother has eaten something. Tell her this from me: we'll bring the children home!"

The men laughed at this dig at their cowardly friends.

"How can you be so sure we'll succeed?" one of them asked.

"I listen to the birds," Kiongo replied.

"And what are the birds saying, pray?"

"Not to worry. Everything will be alright," Kiongo said matter-of-factly.

The men looked at each other knowingly. *Queer guy*, they thought.

***

Inspector Omar led the convoy. He asked his driver to climb higher and deeper into the forest—as far as the vehicle would go. Then, when he could not go any further, he alighted, and the other vehicles came to level. They were driven into the bush for camouflage, and two armed officers were detailed to watch over them. Splitting into two groups, the rest of the team proceeded on foot, seemingly melting into the brush. Mumbi, Karoki, and Mwenda led the team through the shortcut that Ignatius had shown them.

It was around noon, and the forest was teeming with life. A herd of buffaloes, grazing placidly nearby, looked up. A stocky bull watched the men for a moment. Its neck muscles bulged powerfully beneath its glistening fur. A milk-white egret was perched on its massive hump. The bull snorted threateningly and started digging up the earth with its hooves and horns, making low bellows, warming up for a fight. The egret shrieked and took to the air. Two policemen cocked their guns in case the massive bull charged.

Meanwhile, Inspector Omar's team made a detour around the herd. High up in the trees, a Columbus monkey watched the team pass by. It knew they would be trouble in the forest. Alarmed, the monkey leaped, floating like a glider from tree to tree and disappeared. Karoki whistled his delight at the sight of the reclusive monkey. It looked like a bush sage with its magnificent white mane and flowing white tail.

Trudging at the head of his small squad, Kiongo had not gone far when, suddenly, a bush metamorphosed before his very eyes and turned into a man. Kiongo froze in his tracks but only for a moment. The strange man before him was in jungle fatigues and a red beret. He was tall, lean, and sand-complexioned. Rearing up to attack, Kiongo swung his machete and charged at the man.

A shot rang out. The bullet went wheezing dangerously close over Kiongo's head, and the man growled, "Kenya police! Drop that thing or else!"

Kiongo let his machete fall to the ground. His men followed suit.

"You can't fight the government with machetes," the man said. It was clear he thought Kiongo and his men were part of the forest thugs. "That's a bit reckless. Don't you think?" He asked.

"How do we know that you're really the police?" Kiongo retorted.

Inspector Omar flashed his police badge and smiled as the other policemen appeared beside him.

"My name is Inspector Omar," he said. "And who are you, dude? What are you guys doing in the forest?"

"I'm Kiongo. We're looking for some youths from our village," Kiongo answered for his friends.

Just then, Mumbi and Mwenda came up behind the policemen.

"Enemies or friends?" Inspector Omar asked them.

"Friends!" Mumbi and Mwenda cried out in unison.

"Mumbi!" Kiongo exclaimed. "You gave us such a scare. How could you just disappear like that? What happened?"

"I was kidnapped."

"I thought so!" Kiongo cried. "By whom?"

Mumbi pointed at Ignatius, who was standing just behind Inspector Omar and said, "By this guy!"

Kiongo looked confused.

"And are you sure you're safe?" he asked doubtfully.

"Yes!"

"Don't worry, my friend. The maiden is safe," Inspector Omar said.

Mumbi and Mwenda were so excited to see their fellow village-mates. Inspector Omar allowed them time to catch up.

After a while, Kiongo sidled up to Ignatius and scowled, "What were you up to, dude, kidnapping her?"

"It's the devil, brother," Ignatius said. "The devil, I swear!"

"And what business do you and your devil have to do with the police, eh? Why are you not in jail?"

"It's a long story, brother," Ignatius said.

"You should thank your lucky stars that the police are here," Kiongo said. "Otherwise . . . otherwise, you'd have tasted this," he added and showed his machete.

Inspector Omar, who had heard everything, interjected, "I see you're a gallant man, but of course, I'd have had you hunted down and thrown to jail."

"I come from a village of gallant men and women," Kiongo said.

Inspector Omar smiled. "For now, we are all on the same mission. Everything else will be sorted out after this," he said. "What we need to do is put our heads together and plan our next course of action."

Then Inspector Omar called D.O. Simatei, who had taken a different route with another team. By the time he arrived, the D.O. had another band of villagers along with him. He had bumped into the deserters from Kiongo's band and arrested them. The men were crestfallen with shame when they rejoined their friends.

"Welcome back, guys, but you've given our village a fantastically bad name," Kiongo said. "We shall surely revisit when we get back home," he added, ominously.

"Just make sure not to do anything you would not like me to know," Inspector Omar said.

There was a total of fifty armed men altogether: the villagers with their machetes and the policemen with their sophisticated automatic pistols and guns. After some consultations with Ignatius and the D.O., Inspector Omar announced that they were going to raid the marijuana farms. He divided the villagers up into five corps of six men each. To each group, he assigned four policemen. Nobody was without a role. The farms were going to be invaded simultaneously, to avoid the thugs ganging up on them all.

"And remember," D.O. Simatei said as all the teams dispersed, "We must also make sure we uproot the bhang. By the time we're through, not a single plant should be left standing, even if it means us spending the night here!"

"Yes, I almost forgot about that!" Inspector Omar agreed. He wished the five squads well and sent them on their way.

By a happy coincidence, Mumbi and Amos found themselves on Chief Inspector Omar's team. The farm they targeted was the furthest away, but Omar was such a fast walker that it was all they could do just to keep up with him. His gun drawn while skirting around Black Devil's farm, Chief Inspector Omar led his team throughout the labyrinth of brush, walking as if on padded feet, like a leopard on the prowl. They walked for a good half an hour. Then, across a stream that separated Black Devil's estate from the next farm, they crossed into the next farm. A buffer of ancient trees separated the two farms. Lying flat on the ground to avoid being seen by any sentries, the team crawled to the fringes. Inspector Omar waited for a few minutes to make sure that the other squads had already reached their positions. As he waited, he studied the layout of the land.

After a while, he directed his men to spread out the farm in a huge, half-moon formation. Remaining at the head of the arch, Inspector Omar waited until all the men had taken their places. Then at a signal from him, they started slashing into the farm, destroying and uprooting any illegal crop as they moved.

It was just as they had expected. Wielding machetes and other crude weapons, the farmworkers rushed to protect their fiefdom. Emboldened by the presence of the police, the villagers dug in to confront them. His camera ready, Amos got a vintage point and prepared to record what he expected to be the biggest battle in the forest since the heady days of the Mau Mau, back in the 1950's.

But as soon as the outlaws appeared, the crescent of officers closed around them. Inspector Omar fired a warning shot and ordered the bandits to lay down their machetes. Now in a panic, the thugs turned around to flee. They found themselves trapped in an ever-tightening circle of machete-wielding villagers and armed policemen.

Quite unexpectedly, the men dug in, brandishing their machetes. They would rather go down fighting than allow themselves to be arrested. But as if on cue, several shots rang out. A man cried out—an agonized cry that rang through the forest. Inspector Omar repeated his order. The thugs, seeing that the police meant business, surrendered. Almost too soon, the operation was over. The men were swiftly rounded up. The disappointment of the youthful villagers who had expected something a bit more dramatic was palpable. Kiongo spoke for many when he woefully said, "They should have shot the thugs dead!"

Inspector Omar overheard him and grinned. "I understand your sentiment," he said, "But even a thug has his rights. As police officers, our work is to arrest and prosecute suspected criminals. We are not supposed to be a lynch gang," he explained.

Underneath the watchful eyes of his officers, Inspector Omar immediately put the prisoners to work. They had planted the bhang. Now, he ordered, they must uproot every single stem of the illegal crop. Working swiftly and methodically, the villagers swept throughout the farm, slashing and uprooting as if to vent their frustration out on the luxuriant green crop.

"I wish they'd let us deal with the thugs," Kiongo said.

Another boy responded, "I don't think it would have been worth it. Those poor devils look pitiable. Not at all what I had expected."

"True. You almost feel sorry for them."

"Sorry?" Kiongo gassed. "You forget all the misery they've inflicted on our village?"

"I don't know. I just kind of feel sorry for them."

"Aw, man. Don't be such a sissy!"

"Still, I feel like these fellows are just pawns. You know—minor players in a bigger story. You know what I mean?"

"Yeah, I know. I hear that one of the kingpins was arrested."

"I heard that too. But how likely is it that some lads—unarmed, mind you—could arrest such a dangerous criminal? Something simply doesn't add up."

"Could it be it's all fake news?"

"Maybe."

And so, the chatter continued. The machetes swung, and strong arms worked, destroying and uprooting the illegal weed.

Finally, at long last, the whole plantation was destroyed. Then, all teams met again in Black Devil's farm. Twenty men in all had been arrested on the various farms. The officers, looking stiff and grim, inspected the crest-fallen prisoners, studying and trying to memorize their faces.

"Well, gentlemen," D.O. Simatei said with stinging irony, "We shall ensure that the government gives you a place to rest for quite a bit of your remaining lives!"

"What about the big men? The owners of the farms? We here are all small men, just trying to survive," one of the prisoners demanded fiercely.

He was a small man with a squint. His bloodshot eyes roved around in his head like a chameleon's.

One of the prisoners laughed cynically. His laughter sounded like the whoop of a hyena. Then he started to cough—a chesty, dry, prolonged cough that made tears well up in his eyes. "You make me laugh," he said to the squint-eyed fellow, "The big men were not found in the forest," he said between fresh whoops, "You'll never be able to convince anybody that they are the owners of the farms!"

"This is not about convincing anybody. It is about the truth," Squint-Eye replied adamantly.

"Truth!" the second man exclaimed. He started to cough. When the cough subsided, he finally declared, "The truth is that you and I—all of us—are roasted. Our die is cast. As I always tell you, junkies, this is a big man's world. The trouble is you are all out too cold to understand. But to me, this looks like the end of the road for us, boys. He touched the ground with his finger, licked the soil off the tip of his finger, and, pointing to the sky, said: "The sky-God is my witness!"

Mwenda, Karoki, and Mumbi burst out laughing. That was exactly what Ignatius had done the day before.

It was getting quite late, now. The sun was dipping behind the horizon. In the trees, the birds trilled their odes to the passing of day.

"You're right, boy! This is the end of the road for you!" Inspector Omar said.

Mumbi and Karoki led the police to Black Devil's bunker underneath the stream. Inspector Omar and D.O. Simatei inspected the complex. There were still a lot of files left in the office. The two officers leafed through some of them.

"This is the work of an evil genius!" Inspector Omar exclaimed.

"Yes, a master schemer!" Amos said, gleefully.

This would be his biggest story yet. Already, Amos could see the headlines in the following day's copy of *The Quencher*: *Police Bust Drug Syndicate as Bhang Plantations are Destroyed in Mount Kenya*. This would be followed by his Byline, prominently displayed: *Story and Pictures by Amos Muriithi*. This story, he was sure, would mark his big break! Amos flashed his camera ceaselessly as he gleefully followed the officers from room to room. But in the midst of all these surreal moments, his mind would wander, and he wondered at the pleasant twist of fate that had made his path cross with that of Mumbi in Karatina.

With the inspection over, Inspector Omar and D.O. Simatei decided that some policemen would be left behind, while more would be sent up the mountain to guard the bunker and secure Black Devil's chopper, which forlornly squatted in the glade like some long-extinct primeval beast in the gathering twilight.

"It'll remain here until we take the barons to court," Inspector Omar said. "The judge will decide what's to be done with it."

"If you secure a conviction, the machine will probably be forfeited to the state," D.O. Simatei said.

"Yes. Most likely."

Twelve

When the elders arrived in the village that afternoon, the whole village turned out to meet them. There was an air of dread and apprehension as the villagers gathered in the arena. When all were seated, Mzee Gatama rose to speak. In the manner of the elderly, he did not go straight to the issue that was foremost in the people's minds. He narrated about their journey to Karatina, observing in the process of how the sun had scorched the crops all along the way and how it seemed like this year, there was going to be a drought.

"I don't know what has become of the weather these days. When I was young, we used to have rain all year-round," he said. "But our journey was good as we went and good as we returned," he added quickly, invoking an old warrior's song from the days long before the coming of the white man. The memories of many of his listeners did not run that deep, but the older ones who remembered it from the Mau Mau days understood the insinuation. *There was nothing to worry about. All was well.*

Mzee Gatama talked on and on. And so the villagers listened, some impatiently. It was only respect for old age that stopped the impatient from interrupting the old man.

Then suddenly, Mzee Gatama changed course. "As I said earlier, our journey was good as we went and returned from Karatina. We have returned home happy. We met the district officer. He is a good young man. He listened as he would to a father as we explained our problem.

"But even as we spoke to the D.O., his telephone rang. He picked it up and spoke. I cannot cheat; I didn't understand what he said. He spoke in English and through the nose!" Mzee Gatama narrated. The people laughed at this. The laughter rippled through the crowd like a gushing stream. "He put down the phone and told us that he had been speaking to the police commandant. Our youths were not lost; that's what he told us. In fact, they are over right now at the police station!"

The crowd swayed with excitement. A drone of voices heaved over the arena. *What were the three youths doing down at the Police station? Were they arrested? What had they done?* These questions were being thrown around, and opinions offered. Mzee Gatama lifted his walking stick, and silence descended.

"I hear some of you ask if our children had been arrested," Mzee Gatama resumed. "Who said they were arrested? Is it me, Gatama?"

"No!" The answer came back.

"No, I did not say that. What had happened is that our youths had arrested some bad people and taken them to the police station. Bad people. Men who thrive on evil ways! Who had they arrested?" Mzee Gatama asked rhetorically. "Well, they had arrested dangerous bhang growers in the forest!"

The crowd bustled again as the people discussed the dramatic revelation. Mzee Gatama waited for the noise to ebb.

"The matter is now with the government. I will not say anything more about it," he said, quietly. "You all know how dangerous those drug barons are, and I do not want to be the mouth that ate itself. All I want to say is that our children are fine. The D.O. himself said that he'd make sure that they arrive home safely. So, let's wait and let nobody worry. The children are safe. I saw them with my own two eyes."

That was all the news anybody needed to hold a party. For the first time in two days, Grandmother broke her fast, and though frail, she still managed to join the villagers at the moonlight dance that evening.

***

That evening, when Inspector Omar Hassan and his convoy reached Karatina town, Amos Muriithi jumped off the vehicle. He rushed into his bureau office and immediately placed a call to *The Quencher's* editorial offices in Nairobi.

"Hello . . . This is Amos," he said breathlessly when the secretary answered the phone.

"Amos?"

"Yes. *The Quencher's* correspondent in Karatina."

"Oh, how are you, Amos? Has an Unidentified Flying Object landed in Karatina, or what is it? You sound like you've been running."

"Oh no, Alice," Amos said. "I've just hit the jackpot with the biggest story ever. Just returned from Mount Kenya, where Black Devil, one of the most notorious drug barons in this country, has just been arrested."

"Wow! Black Devil? You mean he's real? A man of flesh and blood?"

"You thought he was a ghost or something?"

"I don't know. He sounded so unreal. I thought he was nothing but a figment of people's wild imaginings."

Alice had worked long enough in the press to know quite a bit about the movers and shakers of the world. The so-called Black Devil was one of them. Ever so reclusive, few people knew who he really was. But his name was whispered in newsrooms and through the streets in awe. To some, he was kind of a folk hero, but a hero they all would have liked to remain in the realm of imagination. The sort of things he was known to do were just too much—too scary.

"Well, he's real. I even have a few shots of him—finally," Amos said. "Is the boss in?"

"Yes, he is in. He's been dictating some memos to me, just now," Alice said.

Amos was not surprised. Phillip Owiti, the Editor in Chief, was a workaholic who was always decrying the lack of a work ethic among Kenyans. As if this failure was a personal cross he had to carry in mitigation for his compatriots, he kept a harsh and punishing work regime.

"Could I talk to him, please?"

"Right away. Let me connect you to his office."

Amos waited. Then without preamble, the boss's voice boomed down the line.

"Well, Amos?" he said.

Amos narrated the whole story to the editor. When he was through, the boss was silent for a while. Then he said, "It sounds dramatic. If you have that story, I'd definitely want to look at it."

"I have it, sir, and it's rather juicy."

"Do you have any pictures?"

"Sure, boss."

"Good, because a picture tells a story better than a thousand words. It's a cliché, of course, but in our line of business, there's no better way of putting it. Email everything to me immediately. I'll wait in the office."

After dispatching his story, Amos felt more relaxed. He decided to go right to the police station to keep tabs on the unfolding story. Back inside, the police station was a beehive of activity. A dozen policemen were recording statements from the prisoners. Inspector Omar Hassan and D.O. Simatei supervised the recording. Mumbi, Karoki, and Mwenda followed the proceedings with piqued interest. Inspector Omar had already informed them that when the case went to court, they would be required to go and give evidence.

When it was Black Devil's turn to give his statement, he adamantly refused to do so. He would not give any statement without his lawyer present. He blasted the police for humiliating him and threatened Inspector Omar with dire consequences.

"We've seen many policemen around here," he sneered. "You'll know who I am. Just wait!"

But Inspector Omar was unfazed. "Take him back to the cell," he ordered his officers.

Black Devil was hauled back to the cell, screaming and threatening Hell's fire on the officers. "You'll regret this, I promise!" He roared.

Then, it was Ignatius's turn to record a statement. Already, Mumbi, Karoki, and Mwenda had told Inspector Omar all that they knew about Ignatius. The Inspector himself took down Ignatius and Japheth's statements. Theirs was an intriguing story. The story of how the former street boy and the erstwhile soldier-pilot had become sapped into the evil world of murder and drug-running intrigued the inspector. As a policeman, Inspector Omar felt that their story, if true, was critical to unraveling the mystery of who Black Devil really was.

"Is Pablo his real name or an alias?" He asked. "It sounds Spanish? Portuguese? I don't know. But it's really such a strange name for a Kenyan."

"Nobody knows his real name," Japheth said. "I don't think he has a name."

"That's not possible," the Inspector said with a chuckle. "It's probably an alias. You know, even the devil goes by many names!"

"It's certainly an alias and, I must say, a not very intelligent one," Karoki said.

"How do you mean?" Inspector asked.

Karoki told him about the movie he had watched a while back about a Columbian drug lord. "It was not just a movie. It was a real story about a real man named Pablo—I forget his other name. He was a drug dealer. I think he was killed in a shootout with police commandos somewhere in the Columbian jungle."

"My God!" Inspector Omar exclaimed. "Then it makes sense. I mean, Pablo must have been his role model!"

"At the very least, it means Black Devil admired him," D.O. Simatei remarked.

"And at the very worst, it might mean our friend has ties with the South American drug dealers!" Inspector Omar said.

"Well, you have your work cut out for you!" Simatei said. "You might have to call Interpol if you're going to get to the bottom of this."

"Whatever it takes, I'm game!"

Ignatius talked like a parrot. He had nothing to hide, he declared, and he was tired of living like an outlaw. Anything else—jail or even death—was better. All he wanted was to salvage his soul. Inspector Omar questioned him closely and took copious notes. And as Ignatius talked, Inspector Omar's heart glowed. His instinct told him that he had a watertight case against Black Devil. If he managed to get this thug nailed, this was going to be his biggest achievement as a policeman. After more than twenty years in service, he would retire on a high!

With all the statements taken, it was time to call it a day. Inspector Omar turned to his young friends. "The villagers must be wondering what happened to you," he said. "I think it's now time you went back home. Otherwise, the villagers might begin to think that something untoward has happened, again."

"Sure," Mumbi agreed. "I'm especially worried about Grandmother."

"Your grandmother?" Amos asked.

"His grandmother," Mumbi said with a laugh, pointing at Karoki. "Everybody calls her Grandmother. She must be fasting and praying for our safe return."

"Interesting," Amos said.

"The elders must have convinced her that we are not lost or dead by now," Mwenda said.

"Well, I hope so," Mumbi said. "But the old girl can be as stubborn as the rock of ages. She'll never be at ease until she sees us safe, back home."

"Rock of ages!" Amos said. "Is she that old, then?"

"She's the oldest person in the village," Mumbi said. "She always fasts and prays if something unsettling happens in the village. She's . . . How to put it? She's the moral anchor of the village."

"Oh, I certainly would love to meet the lady," Amos said. "She must have some very interesting stories. Does she know anything about the Rainbow Dragon?"

"She must," Mumbi said. "She'll tell you about that when you see her."

Amos looked nervous. He was still speaking, but his mind was not in tune with what he was saying. It was as if his mouth spoke of its own volition, saying certain words, while all along, he meant to say something different. *What a shy guy*, Mumbi thought.

"Then you must arrange for me to meet her," he said.

"Why me? Karoki is the best person to do that. She's his grandmother, and he's staying with her."

"Why you? Because I want you to," Amos said. He stole a sidewise glance at her and added, "You know, there's something I've always meant to tell you."

Mumbi felt her heart lurch. Then with a leap, it started racing.

Amos noticed her nervousness. "You know," he said. "I like you, and I'd like us to get to know each other better. I'd like for us to be friends."

"I thought we were already friends?"

"Yes, but I'd like us to be special friends. You know, lovers, kind of."

"Kind of?" Mumbi said, thoroughly enjoying his shyness.

"You know what I mean."

"But you're a journalist."

"Kind of," Amos said with a chuckle. "I hope I'll soon be one—a real one. But what about it? Is it a crime to be a journalist?"

"No. That's not what I mean."

"What do you mean, then?"

"I still have things to do—go to college and become somebody too."

"But you're already somebody!"

"A village bumpkin?"

"That's a very cruel thing to say!" Amos exclaimed. "Listen to this: you are heroine!"

Mumbi smiled shyly. Amos thought that he had never seen her look more beautiful.

"It's only that I made a vow to myself. College first and then all other things will follow," she said.

"That's no problem," Amos said. "Anyway," he added rather abruptly, "Think about it. We'll talk when I come to see Grandmother. Sorry, I've got to run. But it was really nice seeing you again."

"Alright," Mumbi said. *Have I put him off?* she wondered in the same breath.

D.O. Simatei volunteered to drive the three youths to the *matatu* stop on his way back to his station, in his official Land Rover. Inspector Omar hiked a lift to town in the D.O.'s car. But there were no *matatus* at the stage.

"You might as well be my guests tonight," D.O. Simatei offered.

Mwenda and Karoki had no problem with staying over at the D. O.'s residence. But Mumbi was not too eager. She didn't want to prolong Grandmother's fast unnecessarily. Besides, she really needed a proper bath and a change of clothes.

"Then, in that case," Inspector Omar said, "We'll have to drive you guys home."

Thirteen

When Inspector Omar and D.O. Simatei drove the heroic trio into the village, the celebrations had just started. After two days away from the village, Mwenda, Karoki and Mumbi were all happy to be home. But their happiness was nothing compared to Grandmother Rakeli's.

"I think our heroes are finally home," Mzee Gatama said as the green jeep drove into old Rakeli's compound.

"Our *njamba* are back?" Old Rakeli, who was sitting next to him by the bonfire, gasped.

"Looks like it."

The young men, women, the children, and the not-so-old excitedly mobbed the jeep as it came to a stop just a short distance from the elders who were sitting by the fire. The crowd broke into song and dance when Mwenda, Karoki, and Mumbi alighted from the vehicle.

"It's indeed them, our brave heroes!" Grandmother cried.

Suddenly, she was on her feet. It was a marvel just how so fast she was on her feet, leaning on her walking stick and trilling—*trilling* in that same-old way that women these days have forgotten. Silence descended upon the compound. Even the crickets fell silent. Feverish with everybody's joy,

Grandmother unleashed five long drawn trills for each of the boys and four for the girl who everybody had feared lost:

"*Aririri . . . ri! . . . Aririri . . . ri! . . . Aririri . . . ri! . . . Aririri . . . ri!*"

Ringing pure and true with the echo of ages, her shrill voice rippled across the fields and the valleys, filling the whole world with her joy. As soon as Grandmother was through, Mumbi, arms open rushed to greet her. She took her in her arms and held onto her tight. She felt frailer than Mumbi remembered, but the old woman's joy was boundless. Nestling in the warm embrace and giggling like a little girl, Grandmother gasped, "Oh, Mother, it's so good to have you back!"

"Yes, so good. So good to be back, Grandma, and to see you're keeping well," Mumbi cried.

"We feared you might have gotten into trouble in the forest," Grandmother said. "You know, it's not a safe place. Not a safe place for a girl, at all."

"I'm alright grandmother," Mumbi said. She didn't want to spoil the old woman's joy with stories of how she had been kidnapped.

After a while, Grandmother disengaged herself. She held Mumbi at arm's length and looked her up and down as if to make absolutely sure that everything was okay with the girl. Then, quite unexpectedly, Grandmother trilled, "*Aririri . . . ri!*" Everybody turned toward her, surprised. That was the fifth trill for the girl. The old woman saw the quizzical expressions on their faces. She faced the people, and then, something strange crossed her face.

"My honorary mother and best friend, Mumbi, deserves five trills," she said, cockily. "She gets them if I'm the one doing the trilling."

Then, she waited for somebody—anybody at all—to challenge her, but nobody spoke. After an interval, she started to dance, jabbing the ground with her walking stick. Mumbi joined her. Then, Mwenda and Karoki joined them. Kiongo, who had been speaking with Inspector Omar and D.O. Simatei, joined the fray. Then, the search team followed him into the ring. Looking beautiful and sensual in the moonlight, Mumbi danced and swayed. She danced over to where Mzee Gatama was sitting by the fireside and invited him to join them. Ngaita, who was a wizard with the *wandindi*—the six-stringed harp—accompanied them as Mzee Gatama's raspy voice rang out in song:

Be happy all ye friends.
Be happy all ye parents.
All is well. All is well.
Our journey was good as we went.
And good as we returned . . .

When it was over, Grandmother grasped Mumbi's hand and led her aside.

"Our visitors—go to the house and see if there's something for them to eat," she said.

"Alright, Grandma."

The old woman then went to where Inspector Omar and D.O. Simatei were talking to Mzee Gatama. She thanked the officers for returning all *her* children safely back to the village.

"You have real brave children, Grandma," Inspector Omar said.

"We are a village of brave people. We've always been so, ever since the Straightener plucked the magical hairs on the Rainbow Dragon's tail!" Grandmother said cryptically.

The officers blankly looked at the old woman. She smiled and said, "Well, that's a story for another day."

Mumbi arrived, carrying two mugs of steaming sorghum porridge.

"Oh, you need not have bothered," D.O. Simatei said when Mumbi handed over his mug.

"Bothered? Since when did a visitor become a bother?" Grandmother gently admonished.

"Still—"

"Still, what?" Grandmother interrupted. "What kind of a woman would I be? A woman who doesn't offer a visitor even a glass of water. What kind of a woman is that eh?"

"Alright, Grandma," Inspector Omar said, conciliatorily. "Thank you for the porridge."

"It's good porridge. Very good for young men," Grandmother said. With that, her voice fell into a whisper. "You know, I like my young men strong and healthy!" She added with a naughty wink.

"Thank you, Grandma," D.O. Simatei said, laughing.

The old woman winked again and went away, chuckling like a duck at her mischief.

***

That night, Amos couldn't sleep. He tossed and tossed in bed. His mind was rapt with so many thoughts. Phillip Owiti was a demanding editor. There was no knowing whether or not he was going to use his story at all, let alone as a lead. Amos imagined Owiti skimming through his story and trashing it in his characteristic manner. *Oh, what a waste of such a wonderful story. How illiterate!* He angrily said and, without a second thought, ruthlessly and remorselessly threw the precious gem into the wastebasket.

The casket of many a young writer's dreams, the blue wicker basket had a fabled reputation at *The Quencher*. Owiti said the waste basket and the trash bin on his computer were essential tools in his calling as an editor. But to the young writers, the basket was like some subterranean monster, waiting to gobble up their best efforts. There was nothing as mortifying as seeing your hard work crumbled and cast away, just like that. The very thought of it filled Amos with apprehension.

Trash it if you will, He helplessly said. *You could send one of your star writers to do the story, instead. I'll hand over everything to them. Everything. Maybe it's time I looked for something else to do with my life, anyways.* But no, he thought in the same breath. *This is all that I've ever wanted to do. So, I'll hang on until you—or somebody else—opens the door for me. And I don't care what it takes. I'll fight on. Yes, I will!*

It was long past midnight. When he checked his watch, Amos was surprised to see it was almost morning. In another hour or so, the town would stir awake. The roads would bustle with *matatus* and trucks going to the market with fresh farm produce. The newspaper delivery van would arrive from Nairobi with the day's papers. It would finally be time to find out what Owiti had done with his story . . .

Amos turned again and determined to catch some sleep, pulled the blankets over his head. But instead of sleeping, he found himself thinking about Mumbi. The words he had spoken to her earlier came flipping through his mind. *I like you, and I'd like us to get to know each other better. I'd like for us to be friends. I'd like us to be special friends. You know, lovers, kind of . . .*

"What utter baloney," Amos muttered. "What a dumb thing to say to a girl! Really, what is wrong with me? Why not just tell her what I feel and know to be true? Or better still, write it in the soil with my big toe, dumb buffoon that I am. A girl might even find that more charming!"

Now, Mumbi loomed in his mind. In the halo of his mind's eye, she was smiling and looking more beautiful than ever.

"Kind of?" she echoed.

Had that been a sneer in her voice? he wondered, not quite sure if she was laughing at him. But what if she was? *It was my fault, and she has every right to laugh at me,* he thought. *Any girl would laugh at a man so clumsy.*

Amos brushed the shameful and reproachful picture from his mind. Instead, he thought about the story that he planned to write. Not quite sure Owiti would welcome a story about some mythical so-called Rainbow Dragon for his newspaper, he started to think of an angle that would link it to the confrontation that he had witnessed in the forest. *What was it about the Rainbow Dragon and the trio of Mumbi, Mwenda, and Karoki?* he wondered. But his weary mind would not focus, and after a while, Amos found himself thinking about Mumbi again. *Next time,* he said to himself. *Next time . . . I'll . . .*

He awoke to the sun seeping in through the curtains. He quickly jumped out of bed, washed his face in the little washbasin in the bathroom, and without changing from his nightclothes, ran out for the day's newspapers. Even before he reached the newspaper vendor at the street corner, Amos knew something interesting was in *The Quencher.* People stood around the stand, holding copies of the newspaper and talking animatedly.

Then he heard somebody say, "That's the guy, Amos Muriithi. He wrote the story."

Amos felt his heart leap.

"These thugs have been a thorn in our sides for a long time," the man said as Amos came up to the stand. "It's good that you exposed them. We hope the government will now rid us of the menace."

"They will, for sure," Amos confidently said, trying to hide his excitement.

He took a copy of *The Quencher*. His heart leapt again and started racing when he looked at the headline. It was the stuff of which dreams were made. There it was: his story, right on the front page! Feigning a calmness that he did not feel, Amos paid for the paper and left.

Back in his apartment, he read his own story through:

King of the underworld, chief, arrested in the dramatic saga as police bust drug ring in Mount Kenya Forest

Story and Pictures by Amos Muriithi

There was drama in Mount Kenya forest last evening when Karatina Police Commandant Omar Hussein and the local District Officer, Aggrey Simatei led a combined force of police officers and villagers from Hombe village in destroying hundreds of acres of bhang in the forest. Black Devil, also known as Pablo, who is alleged to be one of the most notorious drug dealers in the country, and a local chief were arrested.

The drama started on Friday when three youths from Hombe Village, Mumbi (18), Karoki (14), and Mwenda (14) went missing. Talking to The Quencher *yesterday evening, deep in Mount Kenya forest, Mumbi said she had gone to fetch firewood when a man in a hood abducted her.*

Karoki and Mwenda had gone sight-seeing in the forest when they bumped into Mumbi and the kidnapper. Using a crude gun, the boys were able to subdue and arrest the kidnapper, whose name was given as Ignatius Gitonga.

According to Chief Inspector Omar of Karatina police station, the gun is believed to be amongst those left behind by the Mau Mau fighters during the War for Independence in the 1950s.

Using the crude weapon, the three youngsters forced the man, whose name was given as Ignatius Gitonga, to take them to the bhang plantations, where they arrested Black Devil and his men. Upon asking what led them to risk such a dangerous undertaking, Mwenda told The Quencher *that the spirit of the Rainbow Dragon inspired them. Pressed to explain, the boy would only say it was the spirit of the "Straighteners," who he said are those who want to set things right in the world.*

The boy said that after arresting Black Devil and his men on Friday evening, they held the captives overnight in a cave. Two of the youths, Mumbi and Karoki, went to Black Devil's farm yesterday morning. Assisted by Gitonga, who the youths had somehow managed to recruit to their side, they raided the drug baron's underground bunker, where they unearthed crucial documents.

Yesterday afternoon, the three youths accompanied the police back into the forest. They teamed up with a group of villagers who had gone to look for the lost trio. Together, they raided the other farms in the forest. They destroyed acres of the illicit drug, estimated to be worth over 10m Kenya Shillings. Twenty-five men suspected to be workers in the bhang farms were arrested in the operation.

Both Inspector Omar Hassan and District Officer Aggrey Simatei would not comment on the nature of the documents that the youths unearthed from Black Devil's bunker. The Quencher, *however, can authoritatively report that the nature of the documents is such that if the government decides to get to the bottom of this scandal, Chief Mageca is not the only official who is likely to face arrest.*

Though neither Inspector Omar nor D.O. Simatei would confirm or deny the matter, anecdotal evidence points to the fact that the bhang farmers in Mount Kenya forest are a well-entrenched cartel whose tentacles reach high to the highest echelons of both the public and private sectors.

Speaking to The Quencher *after the arrests, Chief Inspector Omar was confident that all those so far arrested would be aligned in court as soon as investigations were complete. He pledged that the police would pursue and prosecute anybody else implicated in the scandal, regardless of his or her status.* (**Editor's comment: See Editorial on Page 6**)

"Great!" Amos said to himself, marveling at the generous space Owiti had allowed his story. He was so blown away that the feared editor had chosen to editorialize his story.

The commentary was vintage Owiti. In his usual forceful style, Phillip Owiti had titled the editorial: Deal Decisively with these Dealers in Death. It was a call to arms, asking the government to join battle with the drug merchants of Mount Kenya and anywhere else in the country. The editorial raged about the dangers of drug abuse and its impact on the youth: *"The youth of any nation are its insurance for the future,"* the editor declared. *"The government, therefore, cannot and must not sit back and allow a few self-seeking individuals—men who have demonstrated through their destructive actions that they have no conscience whatsoever—to throw the future of a whole nation into the pits.*

"Apart from the destruction the activities of these death merchants visit on the youth of this nation, it has long been suspected that these ruthless drug dealers have been using their ill-gotten wealth to fund the bloody adventures of a horde of illegal gangs. This includes the likes of the so-called Mungiki gang, which has, in the recent past, spread its tentacles like an Octopus and left a trail of death and destruction in the whole of the Mount Kenya region and in such far-flung places as Nakuru and Laikipia in the Rift Valley. The question we at The

Quencher *would like to ask is simple: In the face of this blatant and obvious threat to national peace and security, when will the government wake up to the danger posed by these gangs and their financiers? We believe that we speak for all honest and law-abiding citizens of this country when we say: THE TIME TO ACT IS NOW!"*

Knowing that he would reread the story many times over, Amos decided first to make himself a cup of coffee. The water was just coming to a boil when the phone rang. When he answered, it was Alice on the line.

"Hello, Amos!"

"Hello, Alice. You sound excited. What's up?"

"Are you not excited?"

"You're talking about my story? Of course, I'm happy. It's not every day a stringer leads *The Quencher!*"

"No, I'm not talking about the story, but congrats all the same," Alice said and then added, "Please hold on for the boss."

Amos's heart flip-flopped with—he didn't know what. It was something nameless. A strange montage of fear and expectation.

"Amos?" It was Owiti on the line.

"Yes, sir . . ."

"Well, that was a good story."

"Oh, thank you, sir."

"It could have been better, of course, but it was a good story," Owiti said. "Now listen. We must keep up the pressure on the government to act."

"Yes, sir . . ."

"Listen, I want you to do a feature on those kids. And while you're at it, make sure to find out where they got this idea about the rainbow dragon. If you need help—"

"I'll be alright, sir," Amos said. He wasn't going to let the opportunity to make his mark pass.

"I'm sure you'll be okay," Owiti said. "But don't hesitate to give me a call in case you need any assistance. Can I have the story in three weeks?"

"Yes, sir."

"Good luck. Good day."

And just like that, it was over. It was not what Amos had expected, but he didn't care. Suddenly everything felt alright. Every nerve in his body told him that everything would be alright. No, he need not worry about anything.

All was well.

Fourteen

Co-co, co-co-coo.
Co-co, co-co-coo.
Co-co . . .

Karoki woke up to the call of the Red-Eyed Dove singing. Jumping out of bed, he went to check on his grandmother. She was still asleep. Thinking she must be tired after last night's dance, he decided not to wake her. But as he tip-toed out of her room, she stirred and said, "What's it, my honorary husband?"

"Nothing, Grandma. Did you sleep well?"

"Yes—as good as a baby," she said. "It's been a long time since we had such a good dance in the village."

"Even so, you should not have stayed up so late."

"What did you want me to do?"

"Come in and sleep," Karoki said. "The night was cold."

"Come in and sleep just when the fun was beginning?" Grandmother chuckled. "Is that my Red-Eyed Dove I hear?" she asked.

Karoki knew that the wily woman was changing the topic.

"Yes," he said. "What's she saying?"

"She's asking me why I'm not yet up when the sun's already up!"

"Let me go and chase her away," Karoki said. "You need to sleep in a little more."

"*Ûro!*" Grandmother exclaimed in rebuke. "Is she sitting on your head?"

"Aw, no!" Karoki cried.

"Then leave her alone," Grandma snorted.

Karoki still remembered something she had once said to him. It was a long time ago—long before his grandfather died. His mother had bought some sorghum for them at the Karatina market, and Karoki was helping Grandmother thresh it when birds alighted to feed on the sorghum.

"Let them eat," Grandmother had said, "Or one will perch on your head, and you'll go mad!"

No, Karoki had thought as he ran out of the house. I don't want any bird perching on my head, ever.

It was a beautiful Sunday morning. Peeking between the snow-capped peaks of the great high mountain, the sun glowed bright and warm and soft on the skin. On the ridge of the hills, smoke rose from the roofs of houses hidden behind the trees. It seemed that today, the entire village was waking up late, and people were only now getting the fire going in their heaths.

From her usual perch atop the leafy castor tree outside Grandmother's house, the Red-Eyed Dove sang on. *Co-co, co-co-coo.* For some reason, her rich, sonorous song reminded Karoki of Grandmother's trills reverberating across the valleys and rolling with the hills the previous night. Maybe that's why they like each other, he thought. Perhaps it's because they are both singers.

Everything looked so serene. The events of the last two days seemed almost as distant as the Rainbow Dragon. It was almost as though they had never happened. But they *had.* And thinking about what he and his friends had been through, Karoki was suddenly struck by the stupidity of it all. *What madness had made them take on such dangerous thugs? Why had they so readily swallowed Mwenda's crazy story about the Rainbow Dragon? Oh, I nearly forgot that Amos would be coming to see Grandmother!*

"Karoki!"

"Yes, Grandma?"

"Are you not eating your breakfast, today?"

"Coming, Grandma."

It was as if the Red-Eyed Dove had been waiting to hear Grandmother's voice.

Cooo co-co, it chuckled and with a quick flick of the wings, hoisted into the air. Flapping its wings to a regular beat, the bird turned towards the forest. Karoki watched until it became a small blot in the distance. Then with a sigh, he turned and went in for breakfast.

***

Mumbi had just returned home from church when Amos arrived. In the afternoon, they went to Grandmother's home. The old woman was sitting on a low stool outside her house with chicken chuckling around her as she fed them. Next to her, Karoki watched his grandmother feed the chicken.

When Mumbi and Amos walked onto the compound, Karoki turned to his grandmother. He was going to say something, but the words died in his mouth. The expression on grandmother's face as she watched her chicken jostle for the grains was something he had never seen before. Her expression was that of pure delight—of childlike joy. Karoki could never have imagined anybody could find such joy in such a simple and mundane task.

"Grandma, you have a visitor," he said softly—almost apologetically.

"A visitor?"

"Yes, the man from the newspaper is here. Remember, I told you about him?"

The old woman looked up just as Amos and Mumbi came up to greet her.

"Mumbi," she dreamily said. "How are you, my honorary mother?"

"I'm good, Grandma."

"Karoki did not tell me you were bringing me a friend," Grandmother said.

She looked at Amos. He fidgeted as the old woman brazenly looked him up and down without saying a word. There was something deep and mysterious in her eyes. Amos had the strange feeling that the old woman could see right through him. She seemed to decide that he was alright, for she suddenly smiled.

"What's the name of your friend?" She asked Mumbi.

The way she said *friend* was telling and heartwarming. Amos thought her the most charming grandmother that he had ever met.

"Amos," Mumbi said. "He's—"

"What kind of a name is that?" Grandmother interrupted with feigned impatience. "Is that not the name of that white reverend who told us to close our eyes and pray while his brothers were stealing our land, all over the place?"

"My name is Muriithi, Grandma. Amos is my baptismal name."

"Muriithi," the old woman repeated. "The shepherd. Well, now that's a good name. I'd never entrust my mother to a man with a bad name!" she said.

"No, Grandmother," Mumbi laughed. "It's not what you think. Amos . . . Muriithi is just a good friend. He was with us in the forest. He would like you to tell him about the Rainbow Dragon."

She went into the house and returned with two stools. Mwenda arrived just as Amos sat down, running and out of breath.

"Why do you want to know about the Rainbow Dragon?" Grandmother asked.

Amos explained that he was a writer. And he wanted to write a story about the Rainbow Dragon in his newspaper. He fetched a copy of *The Quencher* from his backpack and showed her the pictures that he had taken in the forest. Mwenda and Karoki could not believe it when they saw themselves in the paper.

"You mean everybody in the country now knows about us?" Mwenda gasped.

"Yes, everybody," Amos said.

Grandmother merely glanced at the pictures and said, "What do you want to know about the Rainbow Dragon?"

"I don't really know. Was there ever such a creature in the first place?" Amos asked. Looking at Mwenda, he added, "Or did Mwenda fool all of us?"

"No, he did not," said Grandmother. "His grandfather was of the generation of the Rainbow Dragon. The spirit of the Rainbow Dragon flows within him. But it was such a long, long time ago . . ."

Then, the dreamy look Karoki had seen in her eyes was back. It was like his grandmother was going before his eyes, slowly drifting into the misty, distant days that she spoke about.

"The country was doing badly with corruption, drought, and the pestilence of strange diseases," she said.

"Then, some young man by the name of Irungu managed to pluck the magical hairs off the Rainbow Dragon's tail, paving the way for a new generation to take over in the ituika—the Great Breaking . . .

"The Straightener, as the young man came to known as, became the forebearer of generations of braves: men, women, and even children. They did not see anything wrong that they did not want to set straight. The country prospered under their rule—until the white man came. And that's when things fell apart again. But the straighteners would not take it lying down. Instead, they took up arms. They did not have much—that's true—but they still had the Spirit, and the Spirit was strong. They fought so bravely that the colonialists had no option but to pack up and leave . . ."

The sun was going down when Grandmother finished her story.

"Interesting," Amos said.

He asked a few questions. Grandmother answered him. When he had no more questions, Grandmother said, "Now, I see the country is not doing so well. Maybe things will change. Or maybe not. It's all up to you. As for me—"

"No. Don't say that, Grandmother," Karoki cried.

"But nobody lives forever."

"Yes, but don't say it," Karoki said. "It makes me sad to hear you say that."

"It's not sad because it's true," Grandmother said. "One day I'll . . ."

"Don't!" Karoki said.

"Alright, my husband," Grandmother grinned. "But as I said, if you think you can fool me, maybe it's time you looked for another wife."

"Thank you, Grandmother, for the story," Amos said.

"Thank you, *Baba*," grandmother said, addressing him respectfully as *Father*.

"Make sure to take good care of my mother and always to treat her right."

"I will—always," Amos said.

For some reason—one that he couldn't fully understand—he felt both happy and a little sad.

"I promise, Grandma," he said.